Totally Entwined Group books by Lori Fayre

Single Books
The Devil's Maverick
The Depths of Time

Unexpected Mergers
The Donne Deal
The Alexander Proposal
The Montgomery Arrangement

Unexpected Mergers

THE MONTGOMERY ARRANGEMENT

LORI FAYRE

The Montgomery Arrangement
ISBN # 978-1-80250-511-5
©Copyright Lori Fayre 2023
Cover Art by Kelly Martin ©Copyright January 2023
Interior text design by Claire Siemaszkiewicz
Totally Bound Publishing

Published in 2023 by Totally Bound Publishing, United Kingdom.

THE MONTGOMERY ARRANGEMENT

Dedication

To my number one fan, Megan.
This one's for you.

Chapter One

July 9

When Paige was working on a painting, time didn't exist. By the time a piece of art was done, she could hardly remember doing it. The feeling was there, and it was easy to look at one stroke of color and say, "Oh, yeah, I was feeling very sad when I laid that down." But she couldn't tell you exactly when it had happened or why. So, when Bryce Alexander assured her that the pieces she'd donated to him were a big hit, she'd had a hard time believing him. Honestly, she couldn't remember which ones she'd picked from storage to send him.

"I'm not kidding," Bryce said through the speaker against her ear. "You outsold everyone else here."

"You know me," she said, trying her best to play it off. She fiddled with a strand of long blonde hair that had fallen out of her updo. "I'm always happy to help. I'm just glad they went to a good cause."

"You could say that," he said. "I've been invited to an afterparty — and I don't mean to brag, but I think some of those girls are really into me."

Paige rolled her hazel eyes. "Not exactly how I wanted my art to change lives." *Leave it to Bryce to turn a charity event into a prime opportunity to pick up women.*

From what he'd told her, Bryce hadn't wanted to go to the event in the first place. Carlton Alexander, wielding his fatherly authority all the way from Greece, had ordered it. Bryce had been getting into trouble lately — and not the kind that was easy to ignore. Over the past couple of years, the Alexanders had become celebrities. Maybe it was because the behind-the-scenes story of Jade and Spencer's dramatic engagement period had gotten out, but it had skyrocketed business and put the family under a new kind of spotlight.

"Aren't you supposed to be cutting back on the partying?" Paige asked, attempting to keep her tone neutral. It wasn't her place to meddle in Bryce's affairs, even if he was her friend.

"Daddy dearest isn't here to enforce that rule," Bryce argued. "Besides, these are art people. Charity art people, to be exact. How wild could the afterparty get?"

As one of those 'art people', Paige knew how wild they could be. Not that he'd listen to her if she warned him… It would only encourage him more. Releasing a sigh, Paige simply said, "Just promise me you'll behave, okay? And don't drink too much."

"Yeah, yeah, of course." His voice became quiet as he moved the phone away from his face, and she knew that some girl in a flashy dress had probably distracted him. "You know, you could always come with me. I can drop by and pick you up."

"That sounds amazing, actually." She leaned against the wall, wishing she could tell him yes. "Maybe some other time, though. I have my showing tonight, and I'll have to be here at least another two hours."

"All right," Bryce said, and she almost thought she could hear disappointment in his voice. "Don't have too much fun without me."

"Talk to you later, Bryce."

"I'll talk to *you* later, Paige," he echoed her words softly.

There was silence before he hung up the phone. Paige sighed again. A night out with Bryce was always a good time, but she had responsibilities. He'd graduated from college only a couple of months earlier, and ever since he'd been free, he'd been an entirely new person. Paige could pick out the signs, the small changes over time, but it was a stark contrast to the Bryce she'd met nearly four years ago. She didn't mind, but he could get carried away very easily.

Paige slipped her phone into the small handbag around her wrist. The night was not about Bryce. It was about her obligations. She'd tucked herself into a corner of the gallery, near an emergency exit, to take his phone call. Behind her, the sounds of the showing could still be heard—the laughter, the clinking of glasses, the music and the critical whispers as people judged the art they had paid a high price to view. It was the kind of thing she dreamed of, but something wasn't right.

Paige didn't feel like herself. Her sleeveless evening gown was expensive, its flowing marbled skirts and cinched waist very stylish without being too eye-catching and flattered her slim figure. Unlike the other artists being featured at Gould's Gallery, she didn't want to stand out. They were all either dressed down for the night or wearing the strangest outfits that had to be impossibly uncomfortable. Normally, Paige would have done the same. Something had changed.

Paige turned her attention to the piece hanging on the gallery's white wall in front of her. It didn't feel like hers. It didn't look like hers from afar. But, when she squinted, she recognized every brushstroke. It was one of her abstract paintings—a large canvas covered with varying strokes of paint, all a myriad of colors blocked off by bold black lines. Each day she would approach the canvas with a new mood, new thoughts and ideas, and paint. As she worked, she would take in the previous day's progress and try to fix it. In the end, it hadn't turned out the way she'd wanted, but she had been well over her deadline, and it would have to do.

"It's beautiful work." Levi Gould materialized beside her. "Though, I don't think you were entirely happy making it."

"I'm not entirely happy standing in front of it," Paige shot back. She smiled, playing it off as humor, but there was mostly truth to it. She had to search hard to find pieces of herself in the paint, and it was a skewed image, blurry like a fogged mirror.

"Are you saying you'd be willing to part with it?"

Paige turned to look at him. Levi was classically handsome with his dark brown skin, neatly trimmed beard and long, thin braids. Like some of the other artists, he was dressed informally, in a T-shirt and blazer, a layered scarf, and white cargo pants with combat boots. His hair was covered with a black fedora, completing his monochromatic ensemble.

They had been friends since college, where they'd taken many of the same classes, but when the time came to choose a career, Paige had stuck with painting while Levi had opened his own gallery. It hadn't taken long for Gould's to become the exclusive art hub in New York City, one that all the up-and-coming artists *had* to be a part of.

Levi quirked an eyebrow at her, his dark brown eyes expectant. Paige realized that she hadn't spoken for several moments, only stared at Levi.

"I'm sorry. What did you say?" she asked.

"Do you want to keep your painting or not?" Levi asked with a smile.

"I'm clearly not married to it," she said with a shrug. "You can keep it."

"I'm flattered that you'd offer, but that's not what I had in mind. You might not be happy with your stunning work, but a patron is." He slipped an arm around her shoulders. "Mr. Talles has made a substantial offer, and I would like to graciously accept on your behalf."

"Hold on. I thought this was just a showing," Paige said, butterflies fluttering in her stomach.

"It is, darling, but that doesn't mean I'm going to turn down an influential collector when he offers my friend five figures. Of course, I would get a ten percent commission since it's my gallery." He laughed. "You're doing pretty well for yourself, aren't you? I think this is the second work of yours that he's bought."

Paige could only nod, still struggling to wrap her head around the five figures part. Between this sale and the success of the charity auction, Paige felt a bit of her old confidence creeping back in.

"Is that a yes?" Levi asked. "Because he would like to take it home tonight."

"He can have it," Paige said, finally shaking herself from her fog. Levi turned away to speak to an assistant, ushering him away once he was done. Paige watched all of it from the corner of her eye, dividing her concentration between the two men and the painting and wondering why anyone would offer so much for it.

"For someone leaving with a considerable check tonight," Levi whispered conspiratorially upon his return to her side, "you don't seem overly thrilled. What is it that has you in such a glum mood?"

Paige smiled at him. "I'm over the moon. I am," she added. "I'm slow at getting used to all this. I mean, I'm used to showings and people buying my stuff, but this is *your* gallery. This is *Gould's*. And it's my first time being here during a showing, so forgive me if I seem a little distant."

"I'm nothing special, Paige Montgomery." He nudged her shoulder with his. "You know me better than that."

"You're special to me." Paige nodded to one of the women holding a glass of champagne and narrowing her eyes at a neighboring piece. "And you're special to the critics."

"I want to show you something," he said, taking her hand. Paige didn't argue, but she glanced around to see if anyone would notice them leaving together. The only person who spared them a look was the assistant placing a 'Sold' placard underneath her painting.

The upstairs of the gallery was roped off for the night. Not even the artists were allowed up until the next morning. Levi had converted the old loft of the building into an art studio where, for a hefty fee, artists could claim a five-by-five or ten-by-ten-foot square to work on their craft. Along with the space, they were also guaranteed exposure on the walls of the gallery once a month. It was a daring business venture, but it seemed to be doing well. A spot at Gould's studio had a waiting list a mile long.

Levi lifted the black velvet rope that led to the stairwell, allowing them to duck underneath. The stairs were narrow, and there was no door at the landing.

When Levi flipped on the fluorescent lights, Paige let out a gasp. She had toured the place, but that had been when it'd been staged for visitors. She knew how chaotic artists' spaces could be, since she had to set one up wherever she was staying.

The loft seemed smaller than it had before, what with all the clutter scattered around. Half-painted canvases were propped on easels and along the wall. Wheeled carts jutted into the aisle marked off with duct tape, signifying whose space belonged to whom. The wood floors were stained with paint and streaks of charcoal. The open space was broken up with the occasional industrial column, but those were splattered with paint as well. It was a lived-in space with a view that most renters would kill for. Despite the chaos around her, Paige had never felt more at home in a new place before.

"We keep our kiln and sculpting equipment in the basement," Levi told her as he led her farther in. "It's been a while since we've had a sculptor rent a spot in here, though." He took her to the tall windows in the back of the room, where the building opened up to the city. Since they were on the Lower East Side, Paige could see straight to the ocean and the Statue of Liberty.

"This is so different from what I remember," Paige finally said. "And it's not at all how it looks in the magazines."

"Are you overwhelmed or disappointed?" Levi stepped up to the window, his tall silhouette set against the lights of the city.

"Neither," she told him. "But I can certainly see why people are fighting for a spot here. I can feel the creative energy."

"You should see it when we're full," Levi said. "It's loud and messy, but it's the best place to get work done.

Though, we do argue about the music from time to time." He motioned for her to join him, and she took slow steps to his side. There was something about him that night, something about the look in his eyes and the way that he spoke. If Paige didn't know any better, she might think he was coming on to her.

"I'd like to see it one day," she said. "I've thought about putting my name on the list, but I don't know if I'll be here when a spot opens up. I don't know where I'll go next, but I've been in New York too long. I'm starting to feel restless."

"What if you could skip the wait?" he asked. "What if someone were to jump you to the front of the line? Do you think that would be worth sticking around for?"

Paige crossed her arms, focusing on the torch in Lady Liberty's hand. "What did you have in mind?"

"One of my artists is going overseas." He said it so casually, as though he weren't trying to offer her a coveted spot at Gould's that could skyrocket her career even farther. "There will be an open easel here if you want it."

Paige turned to him with wide eyes. "I don't think that would be fair to everyone else."

"Being the owner comes with perks, love," he told her. "And I know a good investment when I see one."

Heat rushed to Paige's face as she got the distinct impression that he wasn't talking about her art anymore. "It's a tempting offer," she started, "but, I've been in a creative slump lately, and I don't know if I could make anything worth being on display." She chewed on her thumbnail as she thought. "The one down there must have been a fluke. I don't want to take the spot and not produce anything,"

"It doesn't matter if anyone thinks that it's good enough," Levi said, taking her free hand. Paige could do nothing but watch him as he pulled her closer. "It's the curator's discretion to show what he thinks is worth it. And you're talking to a curator who sees beauty in all that you do, Paige." He surprised her then by raising her hand to his lips and kissing it softly.

So, she wasn't imagining things. Over the past couple of years, what with Jade and Clint in their own separate honeymoon phases, Paige had been spending more time with Levi. And, sure, there had been flirtations, but they were always playful, silly and when they were around other people. It was never something she had taken seriously, but the look in his dark brown eyes warned her that it was time to start.

"Can I have some time to think about it?" she asked, her voice coming out breathless.

Levi smiled kindly at her. "Of course, you can," he told her. "I wouldn't expect you to have an answer for me as early as tonight. How about you get back to me within ten days?"

"Ten days?" Paige balked. "Is that all you can give me?"

He laughed, a low rumbling sound that came from deep in his chest. "I want this for you, Paige, but it's the best I can do. Like you said, there are a lot of people vying for this spot, and it wouldn't be fair to make them wait for long."

Off the top of her head, Paige could think of several reasons to say no. If she worked for Levi Gould, there would always be interviews to attend, photo ops and PR to deal with. And while all of it was good for business, it wasn't her style. Paige liked to travel and see new things. While she would revisit places, she rarely stayed for long.

"New York is beautiful, but I'm not sure if it's the place for me." Having to rent an apartment in the city and take a taxi to work every day... Paige was unsure about a lot, but she knew that anything resembling a nine-to-five wasn't in her future. She smiled at Levi to reassure him. "I'll think about it and let you know, okay?"

"Works for me." He gave her hand a small squeeze and turned back to the window.

Paige took a deep breath. She had ten days to decide if she was going to take a dream job and relocate her entire life to New York. The thing was, she wasn't sure if it was *her* dream — or if it was just what she thought she wanted.

Chapter Two

July 10

It was nice to be back in a familiar place again. The cool marble floors of Alexander International Tower might have been intimidating to some, but for Paige it had become a second home. Ever since Jade had taken up permanent residence in the penthouse, Paige had been welcome whenever she was in town.

Paige pressed the button that would take her to the top floor and leaned back against the elevator wall. Even though the workday wasn't over, Jade had planned to take half the day off. She was always so good about making time for Paige, but this time seemed different. It was like Jade could sense that something was wrong and had sounded strained over the phone. As relaxed as Paige was inside the skyscraper, she couldn't quell the nervous fluttering in her stomach.

Before she reached the top floor, the elevator stopped twice to pick up employees. Every time, she'd smooth down her hair, feeling out of place in her long, purple tie-dyed dress and glittery belt. Honestly, she was just glad that the dress was long enough that no one could see her paint-smeared sneakers. Finally, the elevator was empty and she was taken up to the Alexanders' penthouse.

When she'd first seen Jade's new apartment, she had thought it incredibly bland. Sure, the modern style was all the rage, but it had seemed cold and clinical to her. Over the years, it had changed. Jade had painted navy blue and sage green accent walls, as well as adding new furniture. The living room was no longer sparse or boring but held vases of flowers and picture frames filled with memories. There was still too much white for Paige's tastes, but she was always working to brighten things up, no matter where she was.

She stepped into the penthouse and wandered over to the windows as the elevator closed behind her. The sounds of the city drifted up and made her feel a little less alone. It was a clear day, with only a few clouds dotting the sky. The balcony pool waved in the light breeze and glittered under the sun.

Paige reached up to play with a strand of her hair. She'd always kept it short in the past for convenience, but now she wasn't sure how to cope without it. She'd twirl it around her finger whenever she was nervous, and thinking about her meeting with Jade had her on edge. She wanted to know Jade's thoughts on Levi's offer and Levi in general. She looked out to the horizon, furrowing her brow as she tried to sort through her jumbled thoughts.

Could she truly see herself moving to New York to paint for Levi? That was supposed to be the question she focused on, but another question stood out. Could she see herself painting at all? She'd been in creative slumps before, but something about this one felt permanent. There was no more wonder, nothing inspiring in the world. Maybe the solution was to try something new.

Then there was the question of Levi's motives. He'd clearly shown interest in more than her art. Paige couldn't fool herself into thinking she wasn't into Levi. He was a good friend, not to mention successful and devastatingly handsome. There was nothing stopping her from seeing where that might lead, with or without the job he offered.

Paige had never had to deal with those sorts of decisions. Everything had always been decided for her beforehand. That was something that went along with the family name and, though she was testing the waters to see if she could break from the mold, it wasn't easy to do. She was a child prodigy, wielding a paint brush before she could walk. Everything was laid out for her. All she had to do was go where she was told when she was told.

"You look exhausted," Jade said behind her. "Out late again?"

Paige snapped to attention, smiling wide as she turned to her friend. "It was a long showing last night," she offered. "You know how they can be."

"Don't I ever." Jade kicked her heels off near the elevator and came to perch on the arm of the sofa. "I'm really sorry I couldn't make it last night. I wanted to be there with you."

"You were there in spirit." Paige lifted her arms, waving them above her head. Jade laughed lightly, and it made Paige feel better. If there was one thing she could do right, it was make the people she cared about smile.

Paige could feel that there was something off with Jade. She didn't *appear* different. Her inky hair stopped just at her shoulders, which was shorter than Paige was used to seeing it, and her pale green eyes sparkled like they always had. Paige was envious of that confidence and always had been. Jade was the one who always knew what she was about and was determined to make her ideas a reality. She sat on the couch next to Jade, studying her.

"I'm glad you're here," Jade said, sliding onto the cushion and crashing against Paige, leaning her head on her shoulder. "I could use a friend right about now."

"Does it have anything to do with Bryce?" Paige asked, though she could already guess the answer. "I noticed his name on the trending page this morning. I would like to point out that he wasn't near the top like last time." *Or the time before that,* she added to herself. *Maybe I should have fought harder last night to keep him away from that party.*

"I don't know what to do with him," Jade said with a sigh. "Spencer and I are at a loss. He's been staying here so that we can keep an eye on him, but there's only so much we can do. He's an adult now — past drinking age, unfortunately — and we can't hover too much. But, with Carlton and Victoria overseas, it feels like he's our responsibility."

"Where are they now? Still in Greece?"

"No, Victoria called this morning from Spain." Jade lifted her head to meet Paige's eyes. "She was worried, but we told her that we had it under control. I don't want to bother them. They have enough to deal with, and we promised we would take care of Bryce. They've worked so hard, and I would hate to ruin this vacation for them. I don't think any of us knew how difficult it would be."

"I'm sure they understand you're doing all you can." Paige put a consoling arm around Jade's shoulders and squeezed.

"This all started after he went to college," Jade continued. "And we've been trying to get him to open up about what happened, but he keeps himself cut off. Spencer tried to get on his level the other night. He took Bryce out drinking, and it just ended in disaster...and headlines."

"I remember." Paige said. "I saw the news. You should have known that wouldn't be a good idea."

"I guess we were that desperate. Bryce is like a whole new person. He's always at one party or another, with a new girl every time." She closed her eyes. "I remember when I first came here and saw him after all those years. He was so excited about the future, ready to prove himself and take over his own branch of the family business. Now that he's graduated, he couldn't care less."

There was a long silence after which Jade hauled herself from the couch. "But it should get better soon. We're taking him down to Florida to cool off."

"Florida? Are you going to stay at the old beach house?"

"No, not ours." Jade busied herself with folding a blanket that had been thrown over the back of the armchair. "Mom and Dad moved down there after they retired, remember? We're planning on staying at Spencer's beach house. It's not too far from my parents', so we might stop by and see them."

"Do you think it's smart to send a newly christened playboy to Miami? It's like parties twenty-four-seven down there. You know the crap we got up to, and we were *good* kids." Paige shuddered. "Wait! You said 'we'."

"Bryce wanted to go," Jade said. "He told us it would help to get out of the city. Since the house is on Key Biscayne, he'll have a bit of distance from the major hustle and bustle. Even still, we weren't going to let him go alone, so the condition was that Spencer and I would be there with him the whole time. And, if he messes up one more time...? Let's just say I hope he's gotten it out of his system."

"I'm sure it's some kind of rebellious phase that he'll get over," Paige said.

"Sure." Jade paused, chewing at her bottom lip. "But, between us, I think he's about this far away from losing his place at the company." She held her hand up, her fingers pinched close together. "I didn't tell you this, but Spencer's been training one of his employees to take Bryce's place. If Bryce doesn't straighten up, he's going to put *her* in charge of the European branch.

"Bryce might play it off, but I know that would devastate him. It's what he's worked for his whole life." Jade stared into the empty fireplace. "We'll be leaving the day after tomorrow, and he's made a promise to me and Spencer. We have to give him some kind of trust. I mean, he's twenty-two, not ten, and we have faith that he'll get himself together."

Paige wasn't sure how to take all that. She'd known that he'd changed, but she hadn't been aware of the extent. Bryce was her friend, and she'd been there through a lot, even when he'd been accepted into college. He was ecstatic, jumping in the air and laughing so hard that he could barely breathe. He'd known he would get in, of course, but the email had made it real. He'd been so proud to follow the family legacy, to prove himself to his parents and brother. But now that Paige thought about it, she couldn't remember the last time he'd said anything like that.

"Paige, I'm so sorry," Jade groaned. "You came over to tell me about last night, and here I am venting about my own problems."

"Never apologize for needing an ear," Paige said sternly. "We're here for each other. And my problems don't seem so bad anymore by comparison."

"But you do have them," Jade pointed out, "so talk to me."

Paige took her time, opening the pantry and pulling out a bag of chips. "It's not a big deal. Levi offered me a place at the studio." Maybe if she treated it like it wasn't a pivotal decision in her life, it would seem less daunting.

"Seriously? That's fantastic, Paige! It's just what you've been looking for." Jade beamed with pride as she sat at the bar.

Is it? Paige thought to herself. But Jade was so excited on her behalf that she couldn't ask it out loud. It was her purpose, it seemed, to take a prestigious job. Paige shrugged, arranging her expression into something nonchalant.

"It's a great opportunity," she said, "but I don't know if I'm ready to settle down yet. And I'm not sure about New York, either. It's one thing to visit y'all, but this is something else entirely."

"Well, maybe it's time to settle down," Jade said, leaning her elbows against the counter. "In your own way, of course. And it doesn't *have* to be New York. I mean, I'm married, and Clint's going to make it official with Kindall any day now. And when Bryce gets all that partying out of his system, he'll be moving to Italy."

It was scary when she put it like that. Yes, everyone was settling down, finding their people and their homes. Shouldn't Paige want the same? She was only getting older, but she didn't want to paint anymore. The one constant that she'd had from birth was gone. How was she supposed to know what she wanted out of life? It was too big of a question for her to ask.

Paige sat down next to Jade, ripping open the bag of chips and setting it between them. "There's more," she finally said once she'd worked up the courage. "I think Levi's into me. Like, he might be interested in dating."

"That sounds like a good problem to have," Jade mused. "What exactly happened?"

"He was flirty last night—and not his normal flirty. He was very serious about it." Paige snorted. "I don't know, maybe I'm reading too much into it." She closed her eyes, remembering how he'd held her hand and looked into her eyes as he brought it to his lips. "No, I'm not. He was hitting on me...and very romantically, too."

"Is that a problem?" Jade countered, taking a chip from the bag. "He's gorgeous and sweet and one of your best friends."

"It shouldn't be." Paige sighed and let her head drop to the counter. "I can't seem to get my thoughts in order today."

"I have an idea," Jade said, curving her lips in a way that Paige hadn't seen in some time. It was a smile that always preluded something crazy that was bound to get them in trouble. "What if you bail on this?"

"Bail on what? Responsibility? Life?"

"Yeah, for a little while. Hear me out," she said before Paige could protest. "Bryce is going to Miami to get away from the reporters, right? And we're going to make sure he's okay. What if you came with us? We'd be there for the rest of July. Imagine enjoying this last bit of summer like we used to."

Paige sat back up. She could almost smell the sea water with just the mention of a vacation. It had been tradition for her, Jade and Clint to spend every summer at the Saunders' beach house. And it had been a while since Paige had taken a proper break. "Do you think I'd get in the way of Bryce's…recovery?

"I think some company other than Spencer and me would do him some good. And there's enough space for everyone to have some alone time when they need it." Jade was grinning, becoming wrapped up in her own plan. "This would give you plenty of time to get what you need together and, of course, what you don't bring with you could be left here. What do you think?"

"That works for me." Paige felt a mix of excitement, anxiety and something else she couldn't identify bubble in her chest.

Jade had started to say something when a noise from behind them stopped her. As if on cue, Bryce exited the hallway across from the kitchen, stretching his arms over his head. It hadn't been that long since Paige had seen him, probably a few days, but she was still taken aback. His dark hair was messier than he usually wore it. His light blue eyes were full of humor but rimmed by dark shadows, a testament to his night out. He sauntered into the room, all smiles and cheer.

"Good morning, ladies," he chirped, dragging a hand through his hair.

"It's the middle of the day," Paige said. "Don't tell me you were sleeping."

"How are you not hungover?" Jade asked with a hint of irritation.

"One of the perks of being young, sweet sister." He reached into the bag and grabbed a handful of chips. "Paige, you're looking extra good this morning. Got a hot date tonight?"

"No," Paige said with a laugh.

"Do you want one?" Bryce winked at her, and Paige felt herself blush.

Okay, so maybe there were a few dregs of her old crush floating around somewhere inside of her. And there was last Christmas... It didn't matter. Bryce was her best friend's brother-in-law, which practically made him family. She'd never thought of him as 'family'. More as the cute guy who was way too young for her.

Jade launched into explaining the plan to Bryce. He raided the fridge, nodding and seeming to pay attention to her. Paige, on the other hand, tuned it all out. She pushed any thought of her old feelings for Bryce out of her mind and found herself thinking about Levi again.

She couldn't leave New York without letting him know what was going on. She would be sure to have an answer for him in time, but he had to understand that she needed to get away for a bit first, even if it was only for a few days.

On the bright side, she could have time to clear her head. And a change in scenery might help her out of her creative slump. She looked between Bryce and Jade with a smile. This trip was something she needed but had never considered before. This would change everything.

Chapter Three

July 12

Paige hadn't made a habit of flying in private jets, but whenever the opportunity arose, she was more than happy to take it. She was the first to arrive at the hangar that morning, her two suitcases full of new clothes for the trip. She'd only intended to be in New York for a couple of nights, so there hadn't been much packing to worry about. Paige was the sort of person who owned very little, and most of it was back at her Texas apartment.

Usually, her second suitcase would only hold art supplies. She would have her cases of paints, bags of brushes and jars of thinner safely tucked away. All that had been left at the Alexanders' the night before, and she trusted that it would all be safe while she was away.

For the trip, she was only bringing a sketchbook and a few pencils. It made her feel naked, vulnerable even, like she didn't have everything she needed. Painting was such a large piece of her that, even when she was blocked, knowing that she wouldn't have the option to paint for the rest of the month made her panicked.

It was a warm, foggy morning in New York. She couldn't see the city from the hangar, only the gray mist that covered everything. It was a gloomy start to a vacation, but it wouldn't be once they arrived in Florida. She would just have to hang on until then and ignore any warning signs she saw along the way. Whatever the universe was trying to tell her didn't matter. She was going to have a great vacation, no matter what.

While she waited, Paige pulled out her cell phone. She'd put it off long enough, waiting until the last possible second. Though she didn't want to admit it to herself, she knew that it was to keep Levi from talking her out of leaving. She didn't know if he'd try, but if anyone could, it would be him. Levi picked up on the second ring, and she noted the hopeful inflection when he greeted her.

"Do you have good news for me?" he asked after pleasantries were exchanged.

"I don't have bad news," Paige said. She tried to keep her voice light but failed miserably.

"What's wrong?" There was a rustling as he stood, a sound that Paige caught over the phone.

"Nothing's wrong," she said nervously. "I wanted to give you an update. I'm still thinking through everything, but I thought you should know that I'll be out of town for a while."

"Out of town?" Levi sounded relieved, but slightly suspicious. "What do you mean?"

"Jade invited me to go with her to Miami. It's only for the rest of the month, so I should be back by August. But I promise I'll let you know my decision in time."

There was a long pause after that. It was so quiet that she could almost hear Levi's slow pacing, imagining the soft thud of each step. She could visualize him walking though the studio in his worn-out combat boots, his eyebrows drawn together as he thought about her words.

"I think that's a smart idea," he finally said. "Maybe it'll give you some perspective. I'm kinda worried that you'll lose focus down there. Miami is full of distractions."

The way he said distractions made Paige wonder what exactly he was talking about. Sure, there were distractions in Miami—nightclubs, parties, beaches. But there were more than enough of those in New York.

"I'll be fine," she said, knowing that it wouldn't do much to soothe him. "I'll keep my phone on in case you need me."

"Keep me posted." Another pause as Paige waited. "I'll talk to you later?"

"Sounds good." And, before she could say something she would likely regret, she hung up. Paige couldn't be sure if she had upset him or not. She squeezed her eyes shut. She was overthinking things again. He wasn't upset, and it was perfectly reasonable for her to take the time he'd offered to make sure her mind was clear enough to make the right choices. Why, then, did she feel so guilty?

Spencer's car pulled up only moments after Paige had put her phone back in her purse. Jade smiled brightly at her, closing the door as Spencer came around to join her. He gave Paige a wave before putting an arm around Jade.

For the briefest of moments, Paige allowed herself to imagine Levi doing the same to her. The image in her head was pleasant enough, and she wouldn't mind it becoming a reality. *But is it what I really want?* She would have to figure out if she wanted to take the position at Gould's before she could consider a relationship with Levi. *One thing at a time,* she reminded herself. Paige rolled her shoulders, forcing her mouth into a wide and, she hoped, excited smile.

The last one out of the car was Bryce. He managed to look nonplussed, as though a trip to Miami happened every day. He wore black Ray-Bans, which was ridiculous, considering the fog, and a white button-down that stretched a little too tight across his chest. Dark ripped jeans and his usual Converse sneakers completed the outfit, and he only carried a single duffel bag.

"It's a bit dim out for those, isn't it?" Paige asked.

"Not after the night I had," Bryce muttered before heading up the stairs of the jet.

She turned to see that Spencer, ever the gentleman, was carrying both his and Jade's bags. He hadn't changed much since the wedding. Even though he was past thirty, he didn't appear to have aged a day. He wore his hair in the same cut, with the short, dark locks parted down the side and kept back from his forehead. And his deep blue eyes could devastate any woman who looked into them for too long.

Paige allowed Jade to board before her but wasn't able to follow because of how close Spencer was sticking to her. "Careful," he said, sounding very tired all of a sudden. It wasn't that early in the morning, probably later than he was used to getting up. Maybe he needed a vacation more than any of them.

Jade and Spencer had continued to be that annoyingly loving couple who never quite moved out of their honeymoon phase. They were madly in love with each other, and it was obvious to anyone with eyes. It could wear on Paige from time to time, but she was glad that her best friend was happy.

She followed them inside, handing her suitcases over to the attendant and dropping her bag next to one of the windows. Her intention was to recline in the white leather seat and stare out of the window until she drifted off to sleep. The black jet was number five in the Alexanders' collection of planes, and she could only imagine how luxurious the first one was. Before she got too comfortable, Paige decided to grab a bottle of water from the small refreshment center near the front. The goal was to get up as little as possible during the three-hour flight.

Bryce was there, chatting breezily with the pilots as they prepared for takeoff. He turned to look at her, his award-winning smile lighting up the hallway better than the fluorescent lighting. Bryce and Spencer had always looked similar, though Bryce was beginning to grow out of that. His hair was wavier and his chin sharper. It was his eyes, though, that were different. Their blue was not so much like the deep ocean, closer to the crystal blue waters on a tropical island coast.

Bryce had been on her mind all week and, after her conversation with Jade, she was worried. Still, it was no excuse to compare his eyes to a Caribbean beach. "Feeling better?" she asked, reaching into the minifridge.

"Not at all," he said. "But you gotta fake it till you make it. I'm going to sleep this flight away and, hopefully, be better when we land."

"You and me both." Paige shut the minifridge and held the water against her chest. "Not that I'm hungover or anything." Paige would have been happy to sink into the ground at that point. Why was it so hard to talk to him all of a sudden?

"Not all of us could be that lucky," Bryce said. He brushed past her to get to his seat, his hand resting on her shoulder as he moved. Paige stared after him, wishing she could have another shot at that conversation.

She loved flying, but as the plane's engines roared to life, the weight of guilt threatened to ruin the trip. Her call with Levi hadn't gone as well as she'd hoped, but she couldn't write it off as a disaster, either. There was the temptation to call him back, to make sure everything was okay between them, but she had no idea what she would say. She didn't want to come off as desperate.

Jade sat across the aisle from her, and Bryce took the seat facing her. He buckled himself in and reclined the chair, shoving his earbuds in. He closed his eyes the instant he was settled. Jade produced a book from her bag, and for the first time, Paige noticed that she hadn't brought her laptop. Eyeing her friend suspiciously, Paige buckled herself in, though it would be several minutes until takeoff.

She faced the window and took a deep breath. She was making the right decision. She had to be. Paige shoved thoughts of Levi Gould and mediocre paintings from her mind. She'd think about them tomorrow when she was safely across the country and not able to barge off the plane in a split second.

"Hey, Paige," Jade said. "I'm glad you're coming with us. I know you have a lot going on and it wasn't easy for you."

"It was pretty easy," Paige said. "But thank you for inviting me." She nodded toward Bryce. "Do you think he's okay?"

"Bryce," Jade said loudly. He didn't move. "Bryce, we're being boarded by supermodels. They're taking over the plane." Nothing. "Yeah, he's fine. Probably just worn out from last night. Another club opening but, thankfully, no headlines." She toyed with the closed novel in her hands. "I think you should spend some time with him while we're down there."

"I'm planning on spending time with all of you," Paige said.

"That's not what I mean. I know you two are close, and he could use someone who has his back — someone who isn't trying to parent him like he thinks we are," she clarified.

"We don't talk much about our problems," Paige explained. "I wasn't aware that there *were* problems."

"I know it has to do with college. You wouldn't think a place like Columbia would do that to a person, but it's taken a toll on him. He hasn't said anything specific, but I think he needs a friend. He doesn't have many, and none that I trust. I know it's a lot to ask — and you can say no if you want."

"I would never say no," Paige said. "And, frankly, I'm offended that you think I would. You don't have to tell me to spend time with someone I care about. I'm here for all of you because y'all are doing the same for me." She reached across the aisle and squeezed Jade's hand. "I love you guys."

"And we love you." Jade looked at Bryce, a certain softness in her eyes. "I just don't want him falling into old habits."

Paige couldn't remember Bryce when he was younger. Back when the Alexanders would visit Jade's family over the summer, she'd spend most of her time with Jade and, occasionally, Spencer. It was no wonder that, with the seven-year difference between them, she had never met Bryce until Jade's engagement. Still, the difference between him then and now was startling.

"I think..." Paige stopped, trying to piece together the best way to express his thoughts. "I think that you're right. And I'm here to help however I can." She laughed, only half joking as she said, "I can't solve my own problems, but I'll give someone else's a shot."

"You're the best friend in the world. Did you know that?" Jade squeezed Paige's hand before letting go. "It's strange," she said thoughtfully as the plane rolled across the asphalt. "It feels like the end of an era, doesn't it? We're all moving forward with our lives, moving on and figuring it all out. Even you're trying to decide what comes next."

"You've always had it figured out, though," Paige said.

"Not as much as you'd think. This might be the last vacation we take for a while. It feels like everything's going to change soon, and I think we should enjoy this as much as we can."

Paige didn't have a response. Jade's words sank in, lending a strangely somber tone to the cabin. The plane shuddered slightly as the pilots announced that they would be hitting some turbulence soon. It was something that wouldn't have concerned Paige if she hadn't been so tense. She tightened her fingers on the arm rests, anxiety blooming in her chest. And it would appear that she wasn't alone.

"Everyone okay?" Spencer asked, leaning forward in his seat across from Jade. He'd also had headphones in, but he took them out and placed them back in their case with trembling hands. The shaking could be excused by the turbulence, but his pinched expression couldn't.

"I didn't take you for a nervous flyer," Paige said, mostly trying to ease her own nerves. "Isn't traveling part of your job?"

Spencer laughed but didn't say anything as he pushed himself back into his seat. Something was definitely off with him, and it probably had nothing to do with the flight. Like her, he had a lot on his plate. With Bryce on familial probation, this wouldn't be a vacation for Spencer. Bryce was his responsibility, and he would have to keep him in line. She'd seen how it affected Jade, so she couldn't imagine the weight on Spencer's shoulders.

Paige resolved that she would help as much as she could. She would love to spend more time with Bryce and, if he happened to tell her about what was going on with him along the way, it would only help. She turned back to the window, watching as the fog around them broke. They left the storm behind them and sunlight streamed in through the windows. Paige lowered the shade a fraction.

That was a sign she would be glad to take. The future seemed bright and, if only for that day, she had all the time in the world. It might very well be the end of an era, but that meant something new was about to begin. She didn't know what it was yet, but she had a feeling that the answer would be waiting for her in Florida.

Chapter Four

Summertime in Texas could be literal hell. On those dry days where Paige had grown up, walking outside could take the air out of your lungs. Miami was different. Miami had a humid heat that made you feel like you were sweating when you weren't. When Paige stepped out of the plane, a thin layer of moisture settled on her skin. She pulled her hair off her neck, twisting it with a tie she kept around her wrist.

"Is it just me or does it get worse every time we come down here?" Paige asked. Her T-shirt was already sticking to her back, and she was glad she'd worn cut-off shorts and sandals. If Jade heard her question, she didn't answer.

It had been the longest three hours of her life. Jade had picked up her book and started reading while Spencer had followed his brother's example and taken a nap. While Paige had wanted to join them, she couldn't close her eyes without having her brain kick into overdrive. Instead, she'd distracted herself with her phone, finally finishing a documentary she'd started watching a couple of days before and starting a new show.

Paige breathed in the fresh coastal air. Even though they were at another private hangar, she could smell the salt water and spicy barbeque that was wafting over from the nearby neighborhood.

"Are we leaving it here the whole time?" Paige asked, gesturing to the plane. There was a lot about Jade's new lifestyle that she didn't understand. In the past, they'd always headed south on a passenger plane. First class, of course, but always on a commercial airline.

"For today," Spencer answered. "This is a special community. Everyone here owns a plane, and they were kind enough to let us drop it off for tonight. Tomorrow, the pilots will fly it back to New York." A black car pulled up and the driver got out, dropping the keys in Spencer's hand without a word.

"Fancy," Paige said.

"My parents invited us over for dinner tomorrow night," Jade told her as they slid into the backseat of the car. Bryce, who had been strangely quiet, took shotgun with Spencer. "Since we'll be on the opposite side of Key Biscayne from them, they thought we could do something together. They were excited when I told them you'd be with us," she said to Paige.

It had been a few years since Paige had seen Timothy and Angela Saunders. The last time had been Jade and Spencer's wedding day. They'd always treated her like she was one of their own, and she smiled at the thought of seeing them again.

The drive to the house wasn't that long, and she enjoyed the trip over the Rickenbacker Causeway. When they pulled up to the Alexanders' beach house,

Paige had to blink a few times to make sure she wasn't hallucinating. It was exactly what she should have expected from the Alexanders, but it somehow managed to shock her.

Jade's family beach house was a cute two-story home, made with stucco in a south-of-the-border style. It was all orange tones and black wrought-iron. Then, there was the home before her. It was the epitome of modern architecture. Its square frame was white and silver, with dozens of large, mirrored windows. The building rose three stories high and reminded her very strongly of the first time she'd seen Spencer's penthouse.

"Isn't it great?" Jade asked, leaning over Paige to peer up at the house. "I've only been here once, but it's insanely cool inside."

"It's something," Paige told her, gawking at the sight. She took her own suitcases from the trunk and rolled them up to the front door. She let the others go inside first and followed them. The entrance ceiling was at least ten feet tall, with recessed lights along the span of the house. The floors were made of bright wood and dotted with plush white rugs. Family photos sat on shelves, each in a gold frame against light blue walls.

A modern kitchen with all the latest appliances sat to her left and a sunroom with a hammock was to her right. In the middle of it all was the living room, furnished entirely in white and gold and a step down from the entrance.

"Stunned silent, beautiful?" Bryce asked.

"Beautiful? Like this?" Paige looked down at her torn shorts and paint-smudged shoes. "Your standards must be astronomically low," she muttered.

"Yes, especially like that," he told her. Then, to his brother he added, "What do you think, Spence?"

"Don't call me that." Spencer smacked his palm against the back of Bryce's head. "And cut it out with the flirting. You're here to move past all that."

"It's who I am," Bryce said dramatically. "You can't change that, as much as you yearn to." The way Bryce said it made it sound like a joke, but Paige could hear the underlying pain. It was way easier in person to tell when he was covering up something.

"Bryce, I don't want—"

"Can't you take a joke?" Bryce asked with a laugh. "Jesus, Spencer, there's no reason for you to be so serious. I call my old room!"

"Seriously?" Spencer asked, passing him to get to the stairs. "There are two main bedrooms, and you're telling me you're not going to fight for one of them?"

Bryce shrugged, shoving Spencer as he ran past him. "I like my old room."

Spencer stayed for a full two seconds before charging after him.

"Boys, don't break anything," Jade called after them. "Looks like you can have the other main, then, Paige."

If Jade had never told Paige about any of Bryce's problems, she would have known about them then. From the outside, Bryce was acting the same as always, but there was something hidden. Paige recognized it when Bryce had made his joke. She'd seen it in the mirror. Sometimes, it was easier to pretend that everything was fine.

"Spencer and I will be on the top floor," Jade told her as they walked. "You'll be on the second floor." They wound their way up the stairs, and she paused by one of the doors. "There are other rooms if you'd rather take one of those."

"And turn down a main suite? Are you out of your mind?" Paige pushed the door open.

The room inside was nothing short of magnificent. Tall windows offered a view of the private beach. One of the windows was already open, making the white gossamer curtains flutter and dance in the salty breeze. There was a bookshelf full of antique hardbound books and seashells. A gray, distressed dresser sat beside it, and on the opposite wall was a king-sized bed with blue sheets and a fringed cream-colored blanket. Paintings of different types of fish were framed in gold and hung all around the room.

"There's no way you're getting me out of here," Paige said, setting her bags down on the bamboo floors. The light fixture above her was made to look like white coral. She touched the distressed dresser that was waiting for her to put her new clothes into it.

"We'll be heading into town for lunch in about half an hour, so be ready to go." Jade waited in the doorway, her hand resting on the handle. "I meant it. I'm glad you came with us," she said, giving Paige a smile before shutting the door behind her.

Paige was glad she'd come, too. Even with the awkward atmosphere between Bryce and Spencer, which she could imagine would only get worse over time, she could already tell that this would be her best chance to unwind and think about the future.

"But not yet," she said to herself. She pulled a change of clothes from the suitcase and headed into the attached private bathroom. The shower was, as she'd hoped, enormous. And the warm water was a welcome comfort after a morning of travel. She didn't know why, maybe it was the close quarters, but she always felt the need to shower after a flight.

Paige got out and wrapped an oversized towel around herself, blow drying her hair before pulling it up into a high ponytail. She chose a teal and gray striped maxi-dress that was loose and sleeveless. She took a white belt from her case and tightened it around her waist. She started to reach for a matching pair of white flats, then withdrew.

Sighing, Paige slipped on a pair of no-show white socks and her old trusty tennis shoes. She wanted to be comfortable, and the sleeveless dress was already pushing it. She grabbed her small makeup bag next, drawing a thin line over her eyelid and smoothing gloss over her lips. The only times she bothered with makeup were when she had a gallery showing, so why was she worried about it now?

"There," Paige said to her reflection. "All dressed up for no reason." Tossing the bag onto the counter, Paige flicked the light off and started for the living room.

"That was fast," Bryce said. He was the only one in the room.

"I haven't unpacked yet," Paige said. She looked from herself to him pointedly. He'd changed into a pair of soft gray linen pants and a teal button-down. He'd brushed his hair back, though stray waves fell out from behind his ears. "We match."

Bryce followed her gaze and nodded. "So, we do. Maybe it's a sign."

Paige rolled her eyes, but she couldn't seem to get rid of her smile. She had to admit that he was adorable, even if he was too young for her. He watched her a little longer than she was used to until they heard Jade and Spencer's voices coming down the stairs.

"Ready to go?" Spencer asked.

"Always," Bryce said. There was a thin layer of ice in his voice that Paige caught, one that hadn't been there when he'd spoken to her. Spencer didn't respond, and Jade didn't seem to notice. For the second time since arriving, she wondered how much of a vacation it would be for them.

The car ride was quiet, and Paige squirmed in her seat. This time, Bryce was in the back with her and, while the energy in the car was tense, that wasn't what had her on edge. A trip to get food had sounded good at first, but she was ready to get in the water. Just the sight of the ocean was enough to awaken that in her.

Paige shrank down in her seat, watching the elaborate beach houses and palm trees pass them by. Every now and then, she'd catch a glimpse of the ocean and her heart would start thumping in her chest. There was something about this place that drew her in, and she thought that she could never leave.

They made it into town and Spencer parked the car outside of a restaurant called Artisan. It was a standard eatery that had several customers enjoying their meals outside under the shade of large red umbrellas. Before they got out, Bryce put on his dark shades and a white baseball cap.

"So I don't get recognized," he told Paige.

At first she wanted to laugh, then she remembered how he'd been trending nearly every morning before he'd come to Miami. She'd seen the pictures, and she couldn't blame him. Bryce had celebrity status, and a photo of him in one of America's party capitals would sell for big money. It also ran the risk of a mob during their quiet lunch.

"Let's hope no one recognized any of us," Spencer said, adjusting his own aviators. Jade offered him an apologetic look before they got out. The severity of their predicament was becoming clearer by the minute.

Cold air rushed over the group as they stepped into the restaurant. It was beautiful inside, with black walls decorated in red and silver. On the far wall was an enormous painting. It was of a family, done in an abstract style that Paige favored with her own work. The family wore bright clothes with vibrant patterns that contrasted with the background. The artist's name was engraved on a plaque beneath the art but, squinting, Paige couldn't make it out.

"They highlight a local artist every month," Jade informed her. "They also have local bands in sometimes. It's very focused on the community culture and helping people get recognized."

"It's perfect." Paige linked her arm with her friend's and leaned on Jade's shoulder. "I love it."

"You can thank Bryce," she said. "He's the one who picked it. I think he was researching places to visit last night."

Paige looked behind her to where Bryce was hanging back, separating himself from the group but smiling at her. Rather than respond, Paige swept Jade away to a corner booth. Paige slid in first with Jade at her side, while the boys sat across from them.

"They have vegan options on the menu," Bryce said. He'd taken the spot across from her. "I made sure before we came here."

"I'm flattered that you would remember," Paige said. Really, it was surprising.

The waitress came over to take their orders. She was pretty and cheerful, and Bryce couldn't stop flirting with her. Paige thought she might get a headache from how much she rolled her eyes at his cheesy pickup lines. It didn't help that Spencer and Jade were busy being a couple next to her. They were holding hands across the table and staring at each other like the earth might end without one of them.

"Don't get jealous," Bryce said once the waitress was out of sight. "There's plenty of me to go around." He reached for her hand, but Paige slapped him away.

"In your dreams, playboy."

"Man, it must be nice," Bryce said loudly, his smile wide. "I wish Dad would set me up with someone. Life would be so much easier."

Spencer pulled away from Jade to give Bryce a look. "Dad's not going to set you up with anyone. He knows you too well."

"For the sake of the single people over here, I would appreciate it if you could wait until we're all done eating." Paige took a sip of her water, her throat suddenly bone-dry. Bryce had that tone again, the one that made it clear he was trying to get under Spencer's skin. She'd done her best to diffuse the situation, and it had miraculously worked.

The group settled into casual conversation, and Bryce didn't make anymore smart comments during lunch. Whatever this newfound animosity was, Bryce seemed to be directing it toward Spencer. Something had happened between the brothers, and either Jade didn't know or she wasn't talking about it. Either way, Paige wanted to know more.

There was more to it than college, and Paige was going to figure it out. She had to make sure that all her friends were happy, even if it meant putting her own problems aside and sacrificing her vacation.

Chapter Five

July 13

If there was one thing that Paige could appreciate, it was waking up to a beautiful sunrise. She'd never been much of a morning person. Those who had seen her when she'd first woken up in the past were haunted by flashbacks of her foul temper. But she liked to think she'd gotten better.

It had been about a year since she'd gone on that retreat to Bali. It was there that she'd learned a deeper appreciation for mornings. She considered herself more of a night owl, but she'd created a new routine that allowed her to get up in the mornings without being a monster or relying on coffee. She could now be a respectful human being right when she rolled out of bed — no caffeine required.

Paige stretched and her eyes ached to close again, but she rubbed it away, forcing herself to focus on the view from her window. The backyard was well-manicured, and she could see a swimming pool near the edge of the lawn. The grass then bled into sand, which covered the hill and stretched out into the soft, foamy waves of the Atlantic. The pink and orange sunrise reflected on the sparkling water, and Paige guessed that it was around six in the morning.

It was chilly in the house outside of her warm blankets, so she pulled a cardigan over her pajamas and started for the kitchen. The house was deathly quiet, but a comfortable kind that she enjoyed. Everyone else was probably asleep, but there was comfort in knowing that they were there.

Downstairs, Paige fixed herself a cup of green tea and sliced up some fruit for her breakfast. Spencer had made sure to have groceries delivered the day before so they could enjoy their first day out without having to worry about going to the store. While she ate, she stared out at the beach. The day was full of possibilities, and Paige was ready for everyone to wake up and get started.

Once she'd finished her breakfast, Paige washed her dishes and stepped out onto the back patio, her warm tea in hand. The sun was higher in the sky, and Paige took a deep breath of fresh warm air. She set her mug down, taking off her cardigan and tossing it over a lounge chair. Paige reached her arms up high, purposefully extending her spine in a Sun Salutation.

Morning yoga wasn't exactly a habit for her but, on a morning like this, she couldn't help herself. The night before, she'd fallen asleep as soon as her head had hit the pillow. However, with waking and clarity, she was beginning to contemplate her reasons for being there. Her nerves jittered as the worry sank back in.

Paige closed her eyes, the soft sound of the waves filling her ears as she focused on her breaths. This was what she was there for. She needed to make the right decision, and that wouldn't happen while her stomach was clenching and her hands were threatening to shake. She bent over into another pose and released a long breath as the blood rushed to her head. *My mind is a blank canvas.*

As she moved through her yoga flow, she filled the canvas with strokes of color, each one evoking a different emotion. She painted, and in her mind's eye, saw what she'd meant to display at Levi's gallery the other night. She could see it so clearly in her head, but she couldn't get her hands to bring it to life.

"Well, this isn't helping." Frustration took over, and she straightened. If all she was going to do was dwell on past mistakes, then she might as well go home. She drained her tea and went back inside, setting the mug in the sink. She'd clean it later when she wasn't feeling irritated enough to break it.

She returned to her room and sat on the floor to dig around in her luggage until she found her sketchbook and pencil pouch. She hated sketching on such a small area. Her favorite sketchbooks and canvases were always oversized and allowed her to move freely. Narrowing her horizons might be just what she needed and, as she left, she let the door swing shut behind her. She wasn't thinking about trying to be stealthy when the resulting *bang* echoed in the beach house.

Paige waited by her door, listening as hard as she could for any sign that she'd woken someone up. Since she assumed they were all situated on the top floor, she highly doubted it, but she waited to be sure. She'd hate to be the reason everyone got up early, especially at a time like this.

Once she was sure that everyone was likely still asleep, Paige crept back out onto the patio and settled into the chair she'd thrown her cardigan over. She sat for a moment, watching the waves crash and recede, wondering what she should draw. The sky had lightened to a pale blue, and the clouds had started to drain of color, most of them tufts of cotton in the sky. It was early, but she could already hear neighbors heading down to their stretches of beach.

After another few minutes of thought, Paige moved her pencil over the paper lightly, each stroke bringing something to reality. She had the idea of a woman being tossed in the current, deep under the ocean waves. The woman was being buffeted in a dozen different directions, the waves tearing her apart. She drew the woman with soft lines, making the water around her harsh and dark with sharp, deep angles. Paige was sketching out the hand, the fingers outstretched as though seeking someone to pull her from the depths. It was coming together, and she was sure she could turn her drawing into something real, but it didn't fit the scene around her.

She realized that her new project was too morbid for her tastes. She didn't want to think about what it meant, about how her subconscious was the one controlling her hand. Paige turned to a blank sheet and decided to get some general practice in, lining up the start of a man's profile. She'd never been great at drawing masculine forms, always preferring the curves that came with female art.

As she worked, a new idea formed in her head. Maybe all she needed to get past her creative block was a new medium. She tapped the pencil's eraser against her lips, staring down at the half-formed drawing. An image of her sculpting the man before her popped into her mind. The idea of molding something in her hands, of feeling the clay give under her fingers stuck with her and, suddenly, the pencil wasn't enough.

She decided then and there that she was going to try it. She used to hate sculpting in college. Maybe it was her frustration making all her decisions, but she craved the satisfaction that came with digging her fingers into the wet clay.

She'd started back on the drawing when the sound of the door sliding open startled her. Bryce had come out to join her on the patio. He was in his pajama pants and slippers, with a robe over his shoulders. His hair was tousled, and he shuffled his way over to her with a cup of coffee in his hand.

"Good morning," he said, settling into the chair next to her.

"You're up early," Paige said.

"Not by choice," he countered. "But when people go around slamming doors, it's kinda hard to stay asleep." He leaned in as though imparting a secret. "Our rooms are next to each other."

"I'm so sorry," she said. "I closed the door a little hard, but I swear it was an accident. I thought you were upstairs. I had no idea we were next door to each other and—"

"You're fine, Paige. I was just messing with you." He took a drink of his coffee. "I am glad to have a chance to talk to you, though. Can I see?" He pointed to her book.

Paige had never been timid about showing her work to people but, for some unfathomable reason, she didn't think Bryce should see it. She closed the book and kept it in her lap.

"I'd like to keep it to myself, if that's all right." She drew her knees up. "It's too raw right now, and I wouldn't want you to judge me for it."

"I could never, but I'll respect that." He cleared his throat, looking straight ahead at the pool. It was quiet for a long while, and Paige eventually acknowledged him.

"You said you wanted to talk?" she reminded him.

"Oh, yeah, I did." He cleared his throat again, suddenly appearing nervous.

"Is everything okay?"

"Yeah, fine," he told her in a way that didn't seem fine. "I was thinking about last Christmas yesterday. Do you remember that?"

"How could I forget?" Paige laughed. "We were snowed in the penthouse all day. Flights were canceled and the only place open for delivery was that tiny Chinese restaurant down the street."

"And nothing in Spencer's pantry but booze." Bryce reached over and nudged her. "We both got so wasted that day."

"It wasn't that bad. There were too many more drinking games going on than there should have been." She laid her head back on the lounge. "Is that what you wanted to talk about? Feeling sentimental."

"In a way." Bryce looped the belt of his robe around his hand, a strange thing for him to do. "Do you remember our kiss?"

Paige stopped short. She didn't even breathe. They'd never talked about it after it had happened, and Paige assumed he'd been too drunk to remember. Apparently, he did remember, and he had been thinking about it. Paige swallowed hard. It had been one kiss under the mistletoe, and it had taken months for her to forget how wonderful it had felt, how soft and warm Bryce had been.

"I do remember that," she finally said. "Why do you ask?"

"We've been all right since then, haven't we?" Bryce wouldn't look at her as he twirled the belt mindlessly.

"I'd like to think so," Paige said, her suspicion rising. "I thought you'd forgotten about it, honestly. Bryce, what is this about? You're being weird."

"I was thinking about something yesterday on the plane ride—something I think you would like." He paused, turning those island blue eyes on her. "I have a proposition for you. Call it an…arrangement."

"What kind of arrangement?" Paige asked, clutching her book tighter.

"Now, hear me out, okay? I like you, Paige. You're one of my closest friends and someone I trust implicitly. And I think we could help each other." He took a deep breath, and Paige knew that he was finally getting to the point. "What would you think about hooking up? With me?"

Paige hadn't meant to burst out laughing. She'd tried to hold it in, but it was so ridiculous that it had to be a joke. Nobody came out and asked to have a summer fling. They just happened. "Bryce, you can't be serious."

"Why not? We're both consenting adults. Would it be so weird, considering our past?"

"Don't be so dramatic," Paige said, slapping his arm playfully. "That was one kiss—a drunk kiss on Christmas day between friends."

"Last time I checked, friends don't use tongue." This time, Paige actually slapped him. "I'm only suggesting that we try it out," Bryce said. "A mutually beneficial arrangement that we can call off at any time. And you can say no right now and we will never speak of it again. I swear."

"Where is this coming from?" Paige asked. "We got here yesterday, and you're already suggesting... What *are* you suggesting? That we sleep together? Pretty sleazy, Bryce."

"When you put it like that, yeah, it sounds bad." Bryce sat up, facing her with his elbows resting on his knees. "What I'm suggesting is a casual, no-strings-attached sort of thing. You could even sleep with other people if you wanted. I don't care as long as you're careful and use protection. If nothing else, it'd be something to liven up our vacation. Have you seen who we're here with? They think unpaid overtime is exciting."

"Have you forgotten who you're talking to?" Paige countered. "I'm not exactly a party animal anymore."

"But you're interesting and beautiful and I trust you. I wouldn't do this with just anyone." Bryce checked behind him, as though someone could be listening in. "I can't date down here — or anywhere, really. Between the publicity and Spencer breathing down my neck, it's not like I can go to a club and sweep some girl off her feet. And, no offense, but I can tell you need a lay."

Paige scoffed. "Excuse you," she said, but couldn't argue with him. How long *had* it been? She'd rather not think about it.

"My point is, we could help each other out. We've already proven that we can be close like that without it affecting our friendship. Why not have fun?" When she didn't answer, he continued. "Okay, maybe I'm curious. But I would never try to worm my way into your room under false pretenses. You're too smart for that. For an unconventional woman, I have an unconventional approach. Paige Montgomery, will you please consider being my friend with benefits?"

Paige could only laugh, but she couldn't make herself say no. Why couldn't she say no? "You know that this could ruin everything," Paige told him. "I don't want to put our friendship in jeopardy. I like you too much for that." Still, her mouth couldn't form the words. It was different, especially coming from Bryce, but she liked that he was being upfront with her. Most guys wouldn't have made the effort.

"It doesn't have to ruin everything. Who knows? It could strengthen our friendship. Crazier things have happened, right?"

"And what about Levi?" Paige sat up to face him, realizing too late that it brought them within inches of each other. "You know I'm thinking about possibly pursuing a relationship with him."

"*Thinking* about *possibly*," he repeated. "You're not actually dating the guy and, even if you wanted to, he's a thousand miles away. I'm right here!" He stretched out his arms, his robe falling open. "Come on. After the way you kissed me, you have to be curious, right?"

Paige couldn't stop herself from drinking him in. Bryce was no gym rat, but he was definitely doing something right. His already-tanned chest was broad and defined, with the lightest dusting of dark hair. Paige had once had one-night stands, but never with a friend—and never with someone like Bryce. What he was suggesting would be a repeat engagement, though. He was good looking, sure, and there had been moments of weakness when she'd allowed herself to fantasize about what it would be like, especially after feeling his mouth against hers...

"I think that before I consider this, and I'm not saying that I am considering it," she hastened to add, "we would need to set some ground rules."

"Name them," Bryce said.

Paige scrunched up her nose and thought about it. She couldn't believe she was thinking about it. "For one, either one of us can call the whole thing off whenever we want. No reason, just a 'no' and it's over, okay?" He nodded. "And Jade and Spencer can't know. *Ever.*" She could only imagine what would happen if they found out it was being discussed.

"Is there a reason why they can't know?" Bryce asked.

"If it's as casual as you're talking about, why would they need to? It might cause some issues, and I don't think any of us need that right now."

"Fair enough. It would be best not to traumatize them, as much fun as that would be." He grinned. "It's almost like a forbidden romance, isn't it? No one can ever know." Bryce raised a hand to his forehead, leaning away from her. Paige had to fight the urge to shove him over.

"As long as we don't die in the end. And my final rule" — Paige waited until Bryce had righted himself — "is that absolutely no feelings can be involved."

"Duh," Bryce said. "What do you think 'casual' means?"

Paige couldn't tell him the truth — that her own feelings could be the ones to get in the way. She'd had a thing for Bryce that she'd fought hard to get over. What would happen if she was the one to become attached? What if she was the one to be devastated when Bryce called it off? No, that rule was mostly for herself. No emotions could come into the picture.

"I'll think about it," she said, adding it to the list of things she had to decide. Levi and his job offer sat untouched on her plate and, of all things, there was a serving of Bryce on the side that she hadn't been expecting. *When did this become my life?*

"Well, I'll leave you to it, I guess." Bryce stood up and stretched, his robe sleeves sliding down well-defined arms and revealing the start of a tattoo sleeve. How had she not noticed *that* before? He left her there, sitting on the lounge chair with her sketchbook held tight to her chest. "Hey, Paige," Bryce called over his shoulder. "I could convince you right now if you're interested."

Tempting, she thought before she could control it. No, she wouldn't give in that easily. There were some worrying issues that she would need to sift through before anything could happen. Paige stood, tucking her book under her arm and meeting him at the doorway.

"That's not how this is going to work," she said, her voice barely a whisper. She brushed past him, careful to press her body to his for a second. She got the reaction that she wanted when he sucked in a sharp breath. Apparently, she was surprising them both. "I'll tell you when I'm ready."

It was a new sort of power to walk away and leave him like that, and Paige was aware she could get addicted to it.

Chapter Six

Paige hadn't thought she would need to dress up to visit Jade's parents, but she was very wrong. When she came out in a long white skirt and a green blouse, she found that everyone else had put more effort into their choices. Jade wore a sparkling red dress and Spencer had his button-down shirt tucked into slacks. Bryce looked polished in a similar outfit, though he wore sneakers.

"Is this a formal dinner?" she asked, already backing away to quickly change.

"Of course not," Jade said. She rushed over, taking Paige's hand before she could escape. "You're perfect, Paige. You don't need to change a thing."

Paige didn't believe her, but they were also running late. She wasn't the type of person to hold everyone's plans hostage for the sake of her own vanity. The group left the house, Spencer setting the alarms on his phone as he walked. Once again, Paige was crammed into the backseat with Bryce, which was something she wasn't too happy with.

She was still thinking about his proposition. Though he was offering her a solution to her stress, it had only succeeded in placing more pressure on her. Not to mention, she didn't know why he'd suggested it in the first place or what he would get out of it other than the hookups. And there was a much larger problem. She'd been the one to demand they not get emotionally involved, but it was because of her own conflicted feelings.

Whether or not the happy couple had noticed, things had been tense between Paige and Bryce all day. Paige was trying to keep her distance while she figured everything out. Throughout hours of beachcombing, swimming and board games, they'd only spoken to each other during lunch, and even then it was the bare minimum.

As they all piled into the car, Paige caught a whiff of something that seemed oddly familiar. Clearing her throat, she adjusted herself, discreetly sniffing in Bryce's direction. He was wearing a cologne that she knew. It was Kilian, and she only recognized it because it was the same fragrance that Levi liked to wear. The smokey, refined scent complimented Bryce much better, and it wasn't mixed with the powerful odor of paint thinner.

Paige allowed her thoughts to wander to Levi on the short drive. Whether or not he knew it, he was a part of what was happening with Bryce. And what about the job? Could he have been waiting for her to text him or call, staring anxiously at his phone? No, he wouldn't do something like that. He had far too much going on to care — perhaps once the deadline was closer, but not on an average night.

She took her phone out of her pocket and opened her conversation with Levi. They hadn't spoken since the day before when she'd called him from the hangar. She tapped the edge of her case, wondering what to say. She typed out that she was thinking about him, but that could give him false hope. She quickly erased it, scrunching her face as she pondered. Finally, she closed the app without sending anything and slid the phone back in her pocket.

"If it's that hard to start a conversation," Bryce whispered beside her, "imagine how hard building a relationship would be."

Paige could feel her cheeks redden, and she crossed her arms. "I'll thank you to stay out of my business, Bryce."

"I'm offering you some friendly advice." He turned back to the window, but she could see his smug grin from the corner of her eye.

The Saunders' beach house, one that Paige had spent many summers in, was on the other side of the Key. It was exactly as she remembered, with its orange exterior and cobbled driveway. The Spanish-style villa was set by a marina, with their new boat bobbing gently in the water. There was a fountain and a garden inside the black gates and, somewhere behind the home, the bubbling water of their waterfall pool echoed against the stucco of the house.

Spencer parked the car and they all filed up the pebbled walkway that led to the front door. The lights on the front porch flickered with bulbs that mimicked firelight, and large green plants flanked the entrance.

Jade didn't have to knock before the front door was flung open.

"Jade!" Angela squealed. She immediately grabbed her daughter in a hug as she laughed. Timothy appeared behind his wife, reaching around her to shake Spencer's hand.

Angela and Jade could have passed as sisters rather than mother and daughter. Timothy had contributed very little to Jade's appearance and, Paige noticed, his hair had already grown fully gray and his mustache had extended into a full beard. It aged him, but not in a bad way. Retirement seemed to agree with both of them.

"I see you brought a couple of strangers with you," Timothy said, squinting at Paige and Bryce, who had stayed back in the shadows. He reached out to them, pulling Paige into a hug before passing her over to Angela. "Get on in here, kids. Supper's ready."

Paige let out a sigh of relief. At least she wouldn't have to sit through a public dinner at a nice restaurant. She preferred the cozy, at-home feel to the glitzy places Jade had grown to love. When Angela let her go, Bryce wrapped his arm around her shoulder to lead her in. Paige jumped in surprise but didn't pull away completely.

"For what it's worth, I think you look nice," he whispered.

"Thank you," was all she could say. Had the insecurity been that clear on her face? She looked up, noticing how much taller he was than her. He had to be near six feet, but she'd never thought about it before.

"We grilled hamburgers for y'all," Timothy told them as he led them down the front hall. "Figured we'd eat outside since it's so nice out. And Paige" — he looked back at her as he spoke—"will be happy to know that I got a whole book on how to cook black bean burgers and other stuff just for her. I even cooked them inside so they wouldn't be near the real meat."

"Aw, Dad." Jade slipped an arm around his waist, hugging him.

"Thanks, Timmy." Paige jumped forward to his other side and threw her arm over his shoulders. He hated that nickname, but Paige was the only one who could get away with using it. He'd been a second father to her since she was in middle school, and he'd never objected to it once.

"All right, everyone off." He swatted them away lightly and jogged around the kitchen island to the patio. Angela took his place between the two girls.

"We've set the food up in the kitchen," she explained. "Y'all make your plates, fix your drinks and meet us outside. Paige, dear, you can go ahead and fix your food over there. We have the fan going to get most of the grilling smell away from the house."

"Can I try one of those?" Bryce asked from behind Paige.

"There's a whole plate of them." Angela gestured to the counter where the vegan burgers and toppings had been spread out. "Help yourself."

The rest of the group went outside while Paige and Bryce stayed behind, quietly making their plates. Paige thought Timothy had done a wonderful job, especially for his first time trying something so new. It smelled divine, well-seasoned and was charred to perfection. She put her burger on a bun, topping it with fresh lettuce, tomato, ketchup and mustard.

"I've always wanted to try vegan food," Bryce said with a nervous laugh. "No time like the present, right?"

Paige nodded, turning to where the drinks had been laid out and pouring herself a glass of sweet tea. After his comment about Levi in the car, she wasn't sure what to say to him, and she didn't appreciate that he was trying to pretend like it hadn't happened.

"Okay, what I said earlier was out of line. And I'm sorry." He leaned back, his hip propped on the edge of the table. "You're right. Levi is none of my business. But I do know what it's like to be unsure about someone and, in my experience, that's a red flag."

"I'm unsure about you," Paige said before she could stop herself. It wasn't meant as an insult, even though it sounded that way to her ears.

"Oh, I am definitely a red flag," he said with a laugh. "That's why I'm asking for sex and not taking you out to dinner. God help the woman who thinks I'm a catch."

His light tone made it feel easier to talk to him. "I'm nervous," she said. "I have a lot to figure out, and I want to take my time before I rush into anything."

"That's understandable." Bryce straightened up. "I know I've put new pressure on you, and I'm sorry about that. But I don't regret my offer, and I won't rescind it, either. This is a good idea, and you'll come around to thinking the same."

"What makes you so sure?" Paige asked, picking up her plate and cup.

"I can tell with these things." Bryce followed her outside, whispering in her ear, "How could you refuse?"

His breath was warm on her neck, and Paige involuntarily shivered. He sat by Spencer at the table, leaving Paige with no choice but to sit next to him since all the other chairs were spoken for. Smalltalk dominated the glass-topped table already as everyone caught up.

Paige was glad to hear that the Florida weather had been good for Angela's health, but when Timothy started to talk about stock investments, Paige tuned it out. She loved the man as much as anyone, but business was never something that could hold her interest. In the past, when Jade went on her tangents about how AI was functioning, Paige had to force herself to focus and often failed.

Unfortunately, it was all anyone was interested in discussing. Jade had kept her parents well-informed over their previous visits, so they focused on the newly graduated Bryce. Timothy, being a self-made man, had a lot of opinions about the classes he had taken. Bryce took it all in stride and, though she couldn't keep up with what they were saying, she used it as an excuse to really examine him.

Bryce was different. He wasn't the kid who'd been excited about going back to school anymore. He'd grown up, and Paige wasn't sure when it had happened or how, but she liked it. Why worry about why he'd made his offer, and why not focus on the fact that it was there? She could have this man next to her all to herself, if only for the summer. Wouldn't she be an idiot to deny him?

She was startled from her thoughts when Spencer stood with his glass, his chair scraping the deck. "If I could please have everyone's attention," he said. "Before we leave the table, Jade and I have an announcement to make."

Paige felt her heart seize up, her breath stopping in her throat. Spencer beamed down at Jade, and she picked up her glass of water.

"Mom, Dad," she said. They were both leaning in close, grins splitting their faces. They all knew what was coming, but they were waiting to hear her say it. "You're going to be grandparents."

The table erupted into cheers and squeals. Paige could only stare down at her plate. All at once, everything made sense. How could she not have seen it before? Spencer had been so nervous during their flight, and the pair had been canoodling the whole time. Then there had been Jade's whole speech about the end of an era. Beside her, Bryce was just as quiet.

"Since my parents are out of the country, we called them over video this morning with the good news," Spencer was explaining. "I hope you don't mind."

"Why would we mind?" Timothy asked, his cheeks ruddy with laughter and joy. "We've been waiting for this! How far along are you?"

"Around three months," Jade said, clasping Spencer's hand in hers. "We had some difficulty at first, but we're in the clear. We wanted to make sure everything was on track before we announced it."

"Difficulty?" Angela looked between her husband and her daughter nervously.

"Nothing you need to worry about," Jade assured her. "We're fine now, and everything is under control. I promise."

"Congratulations," Paige finally said, smiling over at her friend. Jade had barely mouthed a 'thank you' before she was set upon by her parents, who were asking her more questions. They all stood, taking their conversation indoors and leaving a dumbfounded Paige sitting alone.

"Paige?" Jade asked, pausing by the door. "Are you all right?"

"Yeah," she said, picking up her plate and starting to clear the table without thinking about it. "Why wouldn't I be? I guess I need to let it sink in. I'll be fine," she added.

"Listen… I know that was a huge bomb to drop. And I know you already have a lot on your mind." Jade sank down into one of the chairs, a light breeze lifting her hair. "You were very quiet at dinner. In fact, you've been quiet since we got here. I don't want you to think I was keeping this a secret from you because I wanted to."

"What? No." Paige sat down next to her. "It's like you said, I have a lot to think about. I'm so happy for you, Jade."

"Because I wanted to tell you the minute I got sick that first morning," Jade continued as though Paige hadn't said anything. "I knew what it was, and my first thought was to call you. I was scared, and I ran into Spencer on my way out of the bathroom and somehow he knew. It all happened so fast." Her explanations were tumbling from her lips in a rush. "We were in and out of the doctor's office, and we didn't know what was going on, but then everything was okay and —"

"Jade." Paige's voice was loud enough to stop her next rant. "You need to breathe. I'm not upset with you, and you don't have to explain yourself. I was in shock, that's all. I know you can't tell by looking at me, but I am over the moon about this. I get to be a cool aunt who spoils your baby!"

Paige leaned over and kissed Jade's forehead, a bittersweet motion that threatened to bring tears to her eyes. She was so happy about the new development, but there was sadness, too. It was selfish of her, but a baby would change things forever.

"That's good," Jade told her. "Because Spencer and I were hoping that you would be our baby's godmother. Spencer is asking Bryce to be the godfather right now, under the condition that he straightens out first. You don't have to do it if you don't want to, though. I would completely understand."

"Are you kidding?" Paige took Jade's hands in her own. "I would be honored to be their godmother," she said, trying to blink away those damned tears that wouldn't stay put. "I'm sorry if I don't seem supportive. You blindsided us out here."

Paige was truly happy for Jade as they laughed together. It was something that she'd always talked about, but she had been worried about having to choose between motherhood and her job. But, living in the penthouse, she would be able to have both. Jade Alexander had it all figured out.

Angela called the girls in, but Paige wanted a quiet moment to herself. Outside, with the strands of lights and the calming sounds of the marina behind her, Paige wondered if her focus was on the wrong thing. Should she be trying to settle down? She would be turning thirty soon, but she didn't feel like it.

A throb began to build behind her eyes, and she turned her attention back to the marina. She couldn't get swept up in the whirlwind. She'd think about it all tomorrow. For that moment, all she wanted was to be there for the person she cared about most in the world and feel proud of the woman Jade had become. Because, at the end of the day, being there for her friends was what Paige was best at.

Chapter Seven

July 14

It was another beautiful day in paradise. Paige woke with the sun, following her new routine of breakfast, yoga and crying over her sketchbook. She couldn't figure out why she'd thought leaving her painting supplies in New York was a good idea, but Jade had promised to take her to a local art store on the mainland later that day.

By the end of the day, Paige had purchased a complete sculpting kit, several different types of clay to experiment with and all the extra tools she could find. She'd had to fight herself not to visit the store's paint section, which boasted to have every color under the sun.

The clay had sat on her dresser, untouched, throughout a day of snorkeling and tanning. Once all the Alexanders had turned in for the night, Paige was left alone with her thoughts and the new medium staring her down. She was about to tell it off for being so judgmental when someone knocked on her door.

"I didn't wake you up, did I?" Bryce asked when she opened the door.

"No," Paige said, opening it wider. "I wasn't planning on going to bed for a while." It was nearly midnight, so she knew that she should try to rest, but she was curious about what Bryce wanted.

"Yeah, I tried, and I couldn't get comfortable," he told her with a small smile. "Not with everything going on."

Paige nodded, offering, "If there's anything you need to talk about, I'm here."

"Did you know that Spencer asked me to be the baby's godfather?" he asked, leaning on the doorframe. "He told me it would be under the condition that I get my act together. I didn't give him an answer, just told him to ask again if that ever happens."

"*When* that happens," she corrected him.

"I'm tired of the pressure," he said. "People are always tacking conditions on to their offers. They tell me they're doing me a favor or helping me out, but I have to do something for them first. And, usually, it's something that goes against my nature."

"I don't think acting like a decent human being would go against your nature," Paige pointed out. "Spencer isn't trying to act right for his sake or the baby's or your father's. He's doing it for you. He wants to make sure you can take care of yourself, Bryce — that you won't get into trouble overseas, where he can't be there for you."

Bryce stared at her before saying, "Do you wanna get out of here?"

"That sounds suspiciously like a line, sir." Paige crossed her arms. "I think I'm going to have to say no. Plus, it's after midnight."

"There's plenty we could do after dark," Bryce suggested with raised eyebrows. "But, if that's not to your tastes, I was thinking about having a bonfire on the beach. There's an old barrel out there that we like to use. We also have the firepit closer to the house, but I like being at the bottom of the hill. It's dark enough that, even with the fire, you can see the stars."

A bonfire did sound nice. Clint would always be the first to suggest it when he was with them, so the thought hadn't crossed her mind until then. She shrugged, leaving the clay where it was, and followed Bryce to the back door. Her cardigan was still on the chair from the morning before, and she pulled it on over her tank top and sweatpants.

There was already a circle of four chairs around the barrel, and she settled into one while Bryce got started on the fire. It was easy to see that *this* was the primary source of late-night fireside chats and that the pit near the pool was solely for appearances.

Bryce pulled driftwood from a pile on the sand and uprooted some dried grass. He threw it all into the barrel and doused it with lighter fluid before striking a match to throw on top of it. The *whoosh* of fire shot up from the barrel as flames curved up to the sky. Paige laughed, gripping the arms of her chair as heat swept over her. It was an unusually cool night, with a cloudless sky and stars sparkling down at them.

"I wish Jade and Spencer were up," Paige said, more to herself than Bryce. "They would love this."

"Oh, they were stargazing from the balcony a little while ago." He nodded to where they could see a glass-encased balcony on the top floor of the house. It was set in front of a darkened set of windows and French doors. "My window was open, and I could hear them giggling."

Paige smirked. "I'm sure they've heard worse when you've stayed with them," she pointed out.

"I wouldn't doubt it." He sat in the chair next to hers. "Can you believe they're having a baby?"

"You're going to be an uncle," Paige told him.

"Don't remind me." Bryce scoffed, then looked over at her. "I'm sorry. That probably sounded horrible. I didn't mean it like that." He took a stick and poked one of the holes on the side of the metal barrel. "It's going to be a lot of responsibility. I mean, being named godfather is one thing, but being an uncle...? That kid might look up to me. And what kind of example am I setting? And all that's *if* I'm in his life. When I move to Italy, I won't be able to see him." He shook his head, tossing the charred branch aside. "It's just one more person in my life to disappoint."

Paige's heart ached for him. She could see the struggle behind Bryce's eyes, the way he hurt. She would do anything in her power to help him if she could. She watched Bryce, the sharp planes of his face illuminated by the flames. He was so troubled, yet so beautiful in the firelight. Paige wanted to reach over and comfort him in some way.

She cleared her throat, staring at the sand as though it would suggest something she could say to comfort him.

"For what it's worth, you've never disappointed me," Paige said. "And I've been around you a lot." She absently rubbed her arms as a breeze penetrated her cardigan.

Bryce breathed out a laugh. "Thanks, Paige. That actually does mean a lot to me." He reached under his chair and pulled out a bag that she hadn't noticed. He produced a blanket and a six-pack of beers, wrapping the blanket around her shoulders and offering her one of the cans. "Your turn. Tell me about what's been happening in your life. I know some about it, but I'd like to hear it from you."

"Thank you," she said, tugging the blanket tight and rejecting the drink. "You planned this, didn't you?"

"I might have wanted to get you alone," he said. He cracked open one of the drinks for himself. "I saw you at the penthouse. That morning when you came by to see Jade and you were waiting for her. I didn't want to say anything and I didn't want to seem creepy, but you looked...tormented." He took a long drink of his beer. "And you were staring at your own reflection, too. I noticed that."

Paige hadn't known he'd been awake. And she hadn't been looking at herself. She'd been looking at the skyline. But, when she thought about it, she couldn't remember the view. She could only remember the fear and conflict in her hazel eyes.

"And, last night, after Jade made her big announcement, it was like you'd seen a ghost. It was the same look as before."

Paige was supposed to be helping Bryce, but it was nice to have someone care, someone interested to know what she thought. Jade had been avoiding it, probably as a courtesy to Paige, to keep some of the pressure off. But how could she tell Bryce that she felt inadequate in every way and that her best friend's happy news had only made things more complicated. She couldn't be that vulnerable with him.

"Someone's acting obsessed," she said playfully.

Bryce put an arm around her shoulders and pulled her close. He stared down at her without a trace of humor and her heart jumped into her throat. "If you don't wanna talk, there are other ways to pass the time."

Paige stopped breathing. Was he serious? And was she seriously considering his offer? Of course, she was. She had been all day. Bryce hadn't cracked a smile to indicate that it was all a joke.

"Bryce, what would you do if I told you no?" she asked. "If I told you that your...idea wasn't what I wanted?"

"I would stop," Bryce said with a shrug. "I wouldn't tease you anymore, but I wouldn't be able to stop myself from flirting with a beautiful woman like you. I might be on the hunt for a hookup, but I'm not going to be a dick about it." He paused, licking his lips. "Are you saying no?"

Paige reached for one of the cool beers stuck in the sand and took a drink. "I really am happy for Jade," she said, trying her best to ignore the butterflies in her stomach. "I'm as happy as I can be, at least. It's hard to be happy for someone who has a map when you're stuck in the middle of the desert." She laughed. "Did that sound as melodramatic as I think it did?"

"Don't worry," Bryce told her, draining his can and tossing it into the fire along with a few more sticks of wood. "I know exactly what you mean."

"It puts things into perspective, I guess. I don't know what I want from life, and I'm wondering if I should strive to be more like Jade. Should I start dating again? Should I give Levi a chance?" She took another sip of her own drink. "Will that affect my work if I take his job?"

Bryce watched the fire, nodding to show that he was listening without interjecting. He pulled out another can.

"I want to talk about this with Jade, but I don't know how she'd take it. I can't walk up to her and tell her that she makes me feel insecure. 'Hi, Jade. Do you think you could put your entire life on hold while I figure out mine?'." She sighed. "I need to handle this on my own. I'll have to find a way to move on."

"You don't have to do it alone." Bryce's hand tightened on her shoulder. "I know I'm not the most reliable person, but I understand where you're coming from."

"Do you mean that?" She sounded hopeful, even to her own ears.

"I know what it's like to feel like you don't measure up. You know who my big brother is. As long as you know that I'm here to help and this offer is completely separate from my other one…"

"Thank you." The only sounds that followed were the quiet rush of waves and the chirping of crickets creating a lullaby that threatened to put her to sleep right there. She had leaned into Bryce, who was staring into the fire with narrowed eyes and pursed lips. She hadn't noticed before, but they were soft and pink in the light. She looked back up into his eyes, surprised to see him watching her with the same expression.

She'd thought that her infatuation with Bryce had passed a long time ago. He was too young, too much of a playboy, and she had other things going on that were more important. She'd never once thought he would feel the same toward her. He was her friend, someone she'd flirted with on occasion but who had never wanted anything serious.

Then again, he wasn't after anything serious, was he?

"Listen," Bryce said, glancing behind him to the house. "If you want, I'll prove it. What if we took a trip to Coconut Grove tomorrow? Just the two of us. And we promise not to complain or try to fix each other for one day. We'll act like normal people and do normal things."

"That sounds suspiciously like a date to me."

"Not a date." Bryce rolled his eyes. "A distraction. We'll make a whole day of it. We can enjoy the beach in the morning and head out around noon when it starts to get hot. I was on some websites today, and I think there's a couple of things in town you'll enjoy."

"Do you think Jade and Spencer will mind us disappearing for a day?" Paige asked.

"I already asked, and they've made plans for tomorrow," he told her. "I was thinking it could be you and me."

Paige didn't know what to say. The thought of spending the day alone with Bryce made her nervous for some reason. Sitting at the fire was the most time they'd spent alone together at once. Or maybe it was because she was sleepy and fixating on Bryce in a way that wasn't entirely appropriate.

"Come on," Bryce encouraged. "I promise it will be fun, and I'll make sure that you don't have to worry about a thing all day." He pulled her tighter, pressing a brief kiss into her hair. "Let someone help you for a change."

It was a personal touch that she wasn't expecting, but he was warm, and she was so tired. Her scalp tingled where he'd kissed her. She questioned his motives for the 'day on the town'. Was it because he didn't want to spend any more time with Jade and Spencer? Or was he testing the waters with her? It could have been a way to get her to agree to sleeping with him.

"You wouldn't try to seduce me on this trip, would you?" Paige rolled the half-empty can between her palms, grasping for any excuse that she could. "I appreciate the attempt at distraction, but I have four more days before I have to give Levi an answer."

"This would be one day," he said. "Maybe we could take the weekend. You need this, Paige. You overthink everything."

"You're right," she said, giving in as her eyes fluttered closed. She was too tired to fight, and another day to think it all through couldn't hurt, could it? "I'll go with you." Finally, her problems didn't seem so big. She didn't panic thinking about the enormous choices in front of her. Even Bryce's offer was seeming better and better with each passing day. She was grateful that he wasn't pushing the idea, as well.

Things were getting better for Paige and, strangest of all, it was because of Bryce.

Chapter Eight

July 16

A sudden storm kept the group inside the next morning. While the wind and rain battered at the house and the waves were tossed high into the air outside, Paige, Bryce, Jade and Spencer all found ways to entertain themselves. They had video games, board games and a foosball table upstairs. It had been Bryce's idea to turn everything into a drinking game.

"That's not very fair to Jade," Spencer had said. "She can't have any alcohol."

"I'll moderate," Jade volunteered. "I might not be able to drink, but I can still mix and pour."

Jade had later added that it was a shame she couldn't partake because she needed something strong to deal with the two brothers. But she did her job and made sure to keep everyone else in check. Paige hated that her plans with Bryce were interrupted, but they were all having so much fun that she couldn't bring herself to complain.

The day had ended with the three of them being absolutely trashed and spread out across the living room furniture. Jade did her best to keep everyone comfortable and rewarded herself with one of her reality TV shows. Though they complained the whole time, there wasn't much else they could do about it, which was probably part of Jade's evil scheme.

It had been nice, even if they hadn't done everything they'd wanted, to spend the day in with Bryce. He was interesting and fun, but he could get carried away sometimes. And he was easy to talk to, despite the seven-year age difference. They'd had no end of enjoyment tormenting Spencer together.

"My God, there's two of them," Spencer had groaned, right before he fell from the couch.

* * * *

Paige woke the next morning with a splitting headache and the sun trying its best to blind her. That was how it was in Florida—storms hit, sometimes without warning, and they could blow themselves out almost as quickly. It wasn't much different from Texas when she thought about it. She looked at the clock to see that it was nearly eleven in the morning. A glass of foggy hangover cure was waiting on her nightstand, along with two white tablets that would help her headache.

Paige popped the pills in her mouth, pinching her nose and downing the murky drink. A little wobbly, Paige stood up and put on her slippers before leaving her room. It was very likely that she was the only one

Lori Fayre

up. She crept into the kitchen, making her tea and oatmeal as quietly as she could. She was grateful that Spencer had thought to stock Paige her very own cabinet of safe snacks and groceries.

By the time she'd finished eating and the kitchen was cleaned up, Bryce had emerged from his room. He was freshly showered, shaved and dressed in a clean white shirt and jeans. His old Converse sneakers squeaked on the tile as he entered the kitchen.

"I see my cure did the trick," he said to Paige. "You'd better go get ready."

"Wait! *You* made that awful drink?" Her mind was bleary and trying its best to catch up. "Get ready for what?"

"I promised to take you to the Grove, remember?" He smirked at her. "I didn't forget. And I already let the newlyweds know that they'll have the house to themselves, so you better hurry before…" He let the sentence hang, but they both knew what happened when Spencer and Jade were alone.

Paige hopped from her seat and hurried to her room to get ready. She hadn't wanted to be the one to bring it up, so she was glad that Bryce had remembered his promise. She was looking forward to a day out of the house, especially after the day before.

She dressed in ripped jeans and a T-shirt from her old college. Again, she had her paint-stained tennis shoes at the ready. She'd learned years ago to dress comfortably for Coconut Grove because of the sheer amount of walking it entailed. She took a zip-up hoodie from her closet and tied it around her waist before braiding her hair in a long side-ponytail.

Without a car of their own, the ferry ride over to the mainland was enough fun by itself. Bryce, wearing his shades and hat, took her below the deck where there was a recreational area with air hockey and ping-pong. Since there weren't many people on board, Paige and Bryce were able to have a few friendly games to themselves before they had to disembark.

Once they'd taken a taxi from the marina to Coconut Grove, they stopped by the shops, browsing through the displays without actually buying anything. Paige didn't mind since they talked the whole time they walked around. Bryce told her about some of his crazy experiences at college, none of which helped explain his behavior but were very entertaining.

When he insisted she tell him some of her own stories, she was more than happy to share about the people she'd met and the places she'd seen while traveling the world. She told him about the galleries and exhibitions and all the unusual food she'd tried. As if fate had been pulling them that direction, they ended up at an informal indoor gallery, where street art was displayed in the open for everyone to enjoy. They took plenty of pictures, so many that Paige was sure Bryce's phone had to be on its last bit of memory.

Bryce had gone to great lengths to find something that fit Paige's diet and was also somewhere she'd never been, so they had dinner at a place called Berries in the Grove. It was the best day Paige had experienced in a long time, and she forgot about every weight that had been dropped onto her shoulders in the past week.

It was late and, as they walked off the rich, delicious food, they watched the city around them light up in the night. One of the buildings ahead was glowing with ethereal, multi-colored neon and it was drawing Paige in. King Unlimited was a new addition to the strip, but it was gigantic. It was clear that the building was a refurbished warehouse, and there was a '21 and Over' sign on the door.

"This looks promising," Paige said. Before Bryce could comment, she'd grabbed his hand without thinking and pulled him inside. The lobby was bare, and there were a few black chairs and a ticket booth protected by plexiglass, along with a wall of square lockers to their left. The walls and floor were black with stars and galaxy patterns.

"Welcome to King Unlimited," a pretty young woman with mocha skin said from behind the glass. She was in her early twenties, with short black hair and tattoos that crept up her arms. Her nametag read T'Keyah. "How can I help you tonight?"

Paige looked over the options presented on a giant chalkboard behind T'Keyah before deciding. "Can we get two of the all-access passes, please?" With those wristbands, they would have access to every activity in the building until the place shut down at five a.m., as well as a voucher for three free drinks each.

While the attendant arranged the passes for them, Paige tried to wrangle her credit card from her wallet, but Bryce beat her to it and handed over his own black card. "I can get it," Paige insisted, still trying to get the card out.

"I told you that you wouldn't have to worry about anything, didn't I?" He grinned at her. "Consider it a thank you for dinner." Bryce turned back to the booth and handed over the card while asking, "So, what's the deal with this place? Based on the lobby, I thought it was a kid's arcade."

"Usually, it is. But we shut it down every other weekend so that the adults can have a fun night out," T'Keyah explained. "It's a pain to clean up after, but" —

she handed Bryce's plastic back to him — "worth it." She handed over the glowing yellow bracelets, two drink vouchers and a set of keys to two of the lockers on the wall. "Y'all have fun."

Bryce and Paige quickly shoved their belongings into the lockers. Paige didn't bother taking her phone in, and Bryce left his hat, sunglasses and jacket behind. It was a bold move, going into what was probably a packed room without a disguise, but she wasn't going to question him. He combed his messy hair back with his fingers and shoved both of their keys into his pocket.

The double doors slid open, flooding the lobby with music and the multi-colored flashes of lasers. The larger bulbs above them were black, lending the dark walls a purple hue. Bryce looked down at Paige, his smile a blinding white in the lights. There were quite a few people in the arcade, but not as many as she'd anticipated, and most of them were in the corner foam pits. A popular song that she'd heard before played over the speakers, but Paige couldn't name it.

Past the rows and rows of arcade machines was a wall that housed several doors and a long pizza bar. There was also a real bar, retrofitted over what was usually the prize counter, where people consumed drinks in every color of the rainbow. The bartender was a woman with long dark hair that was shaved on one side.

"I don't think I'm in the mood for anything strong," Paige said, flipping the voucher in her hand. "Not after last night."

"I'm right there with you," Bryce said. "I'm already taking a risk by showing my face, even with the room as dark as it is. Let's see what else they have here, then we'll revisit whether or not we want a drink." He held out his hand for her voucher and added both to his pocket. "Now, it's a question of what to try first."

Paige began weighing her options. There was not only an arcade, bar and foam pits, but there were doors labeled as theaters, indoor bumper cars, laser tag and a virtual reality gaming center. She was sure there was more, but that would require some exploring.

"How about laser tag?" she suggested. "I haven't played in years."

"All right," he said hesitantly. "But you should know that I'm a very competitive person."

"Then this should be interesting," she said with an evil smile. "So am I."

The door labeled 'Laser Tag' led to a small room with yet another booth. This one had vests and various styles of plastic laser guns displayed behind the large, bald attendant. Bryce and Paige were outfitted with elastic vests that had glowing panels on the front and back. They also got to choose their weapons. Bryce selected a big, intimidating gun with a revolving barrel, while Paige chose something smaller that would allow her to be stealthy and move faster.

"Size isn't everything," she said as the wide doors slid open to a room of flashing lights and fog. Despite the multi-colored bulbs, it was a dark and cavernous room. Paige could dimly make out barriers and fortresses scattered around the floor and, every now and then, the shadow of someone racing past with their bright vest.

"To an honorable fight, Alexander," Paige said, extending her hand to him.

"Don't bet on it, Montgomery," Bryce growled, raising his gun to fire at her chest.

Paige darted away, but her chest plate flashed a red light twice, warning her that she only had two hits left.

"That was a dirty move, Bryce," she yelled, scrambling away and firing wildly behind her as she ran. Bryce cursed, and she didn't have to turn around to know that she'd had her revenge. She leaped behind one of the foam barriers, pulling the top piece of her gun back to charge it.

Someone fired at her from the side, a flash of blue in the fog. Paige whipped her head around in confusion. Whoever it was, they were too short to be Bryce.

"Time out!" she called over the thrumming music. "Bryce, are we supposed to be on the same team?"

There was a beat of silence. "Are we?" came Bryce's confused response from somewhere nearby.

Paige looked down at her vest that was glowing green in a shattered pattern to show she'd been hit once. Or did it mean that she was at full health? If that were the case, shouldn't it have been yellow? "What color is your vest?" she asked.

"Green."

"Mine, too."

"Ours is blue." That time, a woman's voice answered from farther away. "Color indicates your team. When it stays red, that means you're out. Didn't you read the rules? They were posted near the entrance."

Paige held her gun against her chest, trying to figure out where the voice had come from. That changed everything. She peeked over her fortress and saw the towering foam columns and plenty of fog to hide in. The softly strobing lights filled the mist in a mesmerizing pattern.

She gasped as someone leaped over the fortress she was buried behind. She fired once at them and missed, the speaker on the back of her gun emitting a sharp tone. "I could have shot you," she hissed, slapping Bryce's arm.

"But you didn't," he pointed out, a cross between grateful and astonished. "I was right next to you, and you missed!"

"Bigger fish," Paige said, surveying over the barrier again. She hoped he couldn't see the color of embarrassment on her cheeks. Shadows lurked in the fog, but she could guess that there weren't many others in the arena.

"What's the plan?" Bryce demanded, his voice close to her ear. He was pressed against her, one hand on her shoulder, the other aiming his gun ahead.

"You're the one who just graduated," Paige argued. "How about you come up with something?"

"I went to school for *business*. You're the artist, so get creative." Bryce pulled the top piece of his gun back, effectively reloading it.

Paige squeezed her eyes shut. Laser tag had sounded fun, but now she was back under the pressure to make decisions. It might have been different if it was her against Bryce, but she had no idea who else was in the room.

She looked over her shoulder where Bryce was too close. Bryce, who had been so focused on the game, must have noticed that she was staring at him, because he turned to meet her gaze. A plan began to formulate but, before Paige could act on it, a small device was tossed over the barrier. Paige leaned in, reaching for the rubber sphere.

"Get back!" Bryce grabbed the back of her vest and threw her back against the barrier, covering her body with his. A trilling beep followed by a long low beep came from the ball's speaker. Bryce's vest lit up red while her's flashed once before returning to green.

"Was that a grenade?" Paige asked in stunned disbelief.

"You can't let yourself get distracted on the battlefield," Bryce said, his voice low. He was staring down at her as though he were trying to map out her face. She stared right back, not the least bit self-conscious. Without thinking, Paige reached up and touched Bryce's cheek. His lips parted and a small breath escaped.

She wanted to blame it on the game, but the truth was that this was something she'd wanted to do for a while, especially since his offer that morning that seemed so long ago. Bryce leaned his head forward, hesitating only a second before sealing his lips over hers.

As soon as their lips touched, Paige released all her worries and doubts, all of it fading away. There was only Bryce and the flashing lights that somehow penetrated her closed eyelids. She couldn't even hear the music anymore. The only thing that registered was the way his mouth moved against hers, how heavy he was on top of her and how much she liked it.

He wasn't quite the way she'd imagined, in the few times she'd allowed herself to do so. He wasn't rough or invasive. He was careful, testing the waters as though he were scared she would reject him in the middle of his kiss. There was also something else there, something that he was holding back from her. And she liked that, too.

They broke apart at the sound of footsteps.

"You're finished." A woman stood above them, oblivious to her interruption, and fired once to make Paige's vest match Bryce's.

You have no idea, Paige thought.

Chapter Nine

July 17

When Paige stepped out of the salon, she felt brand
new. She'd made the appointment to cut her hair short,
the way she usually liked it, but something had
stopped her on the way over. Instead, she asked if they
could dye it. So, when she was dropped off at the
Alexanders' that afternoon, it was with hot pink streaks
in her long blonde hair.

In high school, she used to love streaking bright
colors through her hair. Then college had happened
and she never seemed to have the time for it. It was a
small thing, but it made her feel more like her old self,
back when she wasn't worried about the future and her
only concern was to enjoy her life as it was happening.

"Aren't you spiffy?" Jade said when she walked in
the door. Both she and Spencer were halfway up the
stairs. "It reminds me of old times."

"I like it," Bryce said, his stare lingering on her too long.

Paige had fought hard *not* to leave her room the night before. The temptation to knock on Bryce's door was haunting her. She wanted to know what might have happened if not for that woman and her untimely attack. She wasn't sure exactly what was building between herself and Bryce, but it had been with them for the rest of the night, during the games and the foam pits and the fun. The way he looked at her, like he'd never seen anyone quite like her, had rooted itself in her mind.

She was overthinking it the same way she had done with Levi, which only led to her nerves squirming. She had to make a decision about his job offer and give him an answer. It had been a little over a week since that night at the gallery, when he'd taken her up to the studio. But what a week it had been.

Jade and Spencer had worn themselves out swimming, so they quickly retreated upstairs for a nap. Bryce was absorbed in the TV, occasionally cutting his eyes over to Paige, but he didn't say anything. Rather than be the one to start the conversation, Paige decided to distract herself with the clay she'd bought.

She changed into old clothes and laid out newspaper on her bedroom floor to keep from making a mess. It helped protect the floors, but her hands and T-shirt were a different story. It would have been too easy to knock on Bryce's door, and it would be easier for him to lead her inside. She had to stay somewhat productive to keep it from her mind, even if it was by turning the newspaper into a crime scene.

She heard a soft knock and knew that it was Bryce before she heard him say her name. She stood, wiping the residue from her hands to her ruined T-shirt before she opened the door.

"Hey," she said. "What's up?" She wanted to kick herself. What kind of greeting was that?

"I was thinking about going into the city," Bryce said. "Do you wanna go with me?"

"I don't know," she said automatically. Behind her, the mottled mound of clay rested on a carpet of newspaper, judging her for considering another activity for the day. "I have plenty to do here, and I just got back from the mainland." She pulled at her hair to remind him.

"Well, we wouldn't be going to the Grove or anywhere else you've been recently." He shuffled his feet. "You've been quiet since last night, and I feel like it's my fault." He started to say something, then closed his mouth before starting again. "Have you ever been to Little Havana?"

"Once, I think."

"I need a break from Spencer. I snapped at him earlier, and I don't know if you could tell, but he's not happy with me. I'm trying to get better, but I can't do that with him breathing down my neck." He looked up and down the hall. "I know you have questions and things you want to talk about. If you come with me, I'll answer anything you want."

"You know, up until you said that, I was convinced that you were trying to ask me on a date," she said with narrowed eyes. Spending another day with Bryce could be wonderful, but it would come with risks. "You do seem desperate."

Bryce shrugged. "I don't like to go out by myself."

"All right," she eventually said. "Let me change first."

"Perfect," he said, that familiar smile returning and making something in her chest flutter. It wasn't a mystery why she felt herself falling for him. Bryce oozed charisma, and it swept her up from time to time. *Like right now.* But it was also why she could never allow herself to start anything, not even a casual relationship, with him.

Once the door closed, she rushed to her bathroom, scrubbing off the clay from her arms. Paige braided her hair back and slipped on a gray cotton dress. Instead of her sneakers, she grabbed a pair of running shoes that still had the tags attached. They were white and chunky and, combined with her oversized white hat, would make her look dressier while still being comfortable.

Paige grabbed her cross-body bag with her wallet and phone, making sure to text Jade and Spencer to let them know that she and Bryce would be out. Jade immediately replied, saying that space would be good for Spencer and Bryce. Paige hadn't noticed anything, but their fight must have been something else. She made a mental note to ask Bryce about it later.

Bryce had already called a cab and was waiting beside it. He'd showered and wore jeans and a T-shirt, but his hat and glasses were missing. It was starting to feel more and more like a date. The house disappeared around the curve, leaving Paige well and truly alone with Bryce again.

Much to her relief, the ride to the docks was quiet, and they were able to board a ferry seconds before it departed. Paige took a spot on one of the plastic benches and Bryce sat across from her, relaxed and resting his ankle on his knee. The ferry was mostly empty, and the sun was well above the horizon.

"You should probably think about what you're going to tell Levi," Bryce said. "You panic under pressure, and if you wait until the moment before, you might make the wrong choice."

Paige huffed a laugh. "You're incredibly invested in this, aren't you?" She crossed her arms and looked down at her shoes, suddenly missing the colorful marks. "If you must know, I'm going to turn down the job. You were right about me not being happy in New York. But I don't have a plan."

"It isn't a bad thing when you don't have a road map," Bryce said. "Hey, as long as you're happy, you're doing something right."

"Well now, Bryce is giving me life advice." Paige nudged his knee with her toe. "Are *you* happy, Bryce?"

He didn't say anything and instead busied himself with putting on his thin disguise.

"Come on. You promised me you'd answer anything I wanted," she reminded him.

"A promise that I'm already starting to regret." But he smiled as he said, "How about we save the conversation for our walk? That way we'll have something to do."

Paige wanted to argue that there was always something to do in Miami, but she held her tongue. She was right, of course, and there was plenty to see on the ride to Little Havana. The village was bursting with life. Cafes were packed to the rafters and, coming through the taxi's vents, Paige could smell the restaurants and cigar smoke. They passed by parks and clubs until they came to a more secluded area. Bryce thanked the driver and paid him while Paige got out.

A live band played in front of a closing farmer's market and there were couples dancing in time. One woman danced by herself, but she was the one captivating onlookers. She wore long, flowing traditional skirts that whipped around her knees as she twirled. Her sandals kicked up dust from the pavement and her long, curly hair swished from side to side. Paige was jealous of the elegant beauty before her, but she couldn't look away.

"This way," Bryce said, taking her arm. "I have something to show you that I think you'll like." He led her away, past more vendors and stores, until they came to a more abandoned part of the town. The sidewalk was littered with cans of spray paint, sheets of newspaper and rags. It wasn't dark yet, but it would be soon, so the road was lined with LED lanterns. About a dozen people were spread out along the road, focused on spraying art onto walls.

Paige watched them work, bringing murals and letters and portraits to life. She wandered around them all, almost forgetting about Bryce. He was standing to the side and nodding encouragement that she hadn't known she needed.

This was art. This was true freedom of expression, raw and unfiltered. Paige stopped by a young boy who was adding details to a portrait. She wondered who the person was and what he might mean to the boy, if anything. The portrait was stylized like a caricature, but with details that should have been impossible to create with spray paint. He stopped and turned to her.

"It's beautiful," she said. "I've never seen anything like it."

He smiled at her and reached down to pick up a can of paint which he held out to her.

"Are you sure?" she asked.

The boy shrugged, shaking the can at her. Paige took it, and he returned to his work. Paige moved to his other side, staring at a small patch of wall that was surrounded by other paintings. It was like a blank canvas meant for her. She closed her eyes, taking in the smells of aerosol mixed with the vendors' wares, listening to the music that seemed to be everywhere.

Without thinking, she opened her eyes and began to move, arcing her arm up and around, losing herself in the moment. She'd used spray paint a few times, but it had been as a base to layer acrylic over. The noise of the street behind her faded away, and all she could see was the painting before her. It wasn't until she felt someone behind her that she slowed.

"The dancer," Bryce said, leaning over her shoulder. His body was close to her, almost as close as the night before. No, he was exactly as close. She could feel the warmth of him against her back, the same as it had been before the laser grenade had landed next to her. Paige lowered the can, willing herself to stare ahead at her creation.

"The music, the food, the life... I felt like she embodied what I'm experiencing. Now, I've immortalized her — at least until the next artist covers her up." The piece wasn't finished, but she was proud of what she'd done. She'd captured the swirling skirt, the motion of the woman's arms as she spun. But it was all blocks and sweeps of color with no definition and, strangely enough, Paige liked it.

"Smile," Bryce said. She had only a second to turn and beam at his phone before he snapped a picture of her with the painting. Then, he came to her side and took a picture of them together. Paige liked the way his arm felt around her. His cologne overtook her and, for just that space of time, she let herself lean into him.

"Ready for some dinner?" he asked. "Or do you want to finish up here?"

"You know, I think I'll leave her as she is." Paige raised her phone and snapped a picture for herself. "Maybe someone will do something more with it."

She followed Bryce down to the strip of restaurants as night set in, and they stopped at one of the smaller places called Slice of Lime. It was crowded inside, but they were able to find a quiet spot at one of the small outdoor tables with a fan circling overhead. They placed their order, with Bryce getting stuffed peppers and Cuban mojo pork and Paige selecting vegan picadillo.

"What was the blowup with your brother about?" Paige asked. Taken with her newfound inspiration, she'd momentarily forgotten their agreement, but now she was determined to hold Bryce to his promise.

"I made a suggestion," Bryce said slowly, thinking through every word. He took his sunglasses off. "There's a new club opening up, and I thought it would be fun to go. Spencer sees it as me falling back into old habits and…well, we argued about it. He tends to smother me sometimes." He looked up at her and she could tell he was uncomfortable. "Is that enough?"

"Yes," Paige said. "Thank you for being honest. I know it wasn't easy. And I understand about the smothering thing. For me, it was my parents hovering over my every move." She stopped as a waiter brought out their drinks. Once he was gone, she asked, "You never answered my first question. Are you happy?"

"Right now? I'm the happiest I've ever been," Bryce said with the most heartbreaking smile she'd ever seen.

"I'm sitting in paradise with a beautiful woman and we're about to be served delicious food. What do I have to complain about?"

"I'm being serious," Paige said with a laugh.

"So am I." Bryce's expression softened and there was something about the look he gave her. It was the same as it had been before they'd kissed.

Paige leaned on the table, focusing on the fairy lights that twinkled along the banisters and the band that was setting up to perform across the street. She'd do anything to keep from looking back at Bryce. As though he sensed that, Bryce stood up and took her hand, tugging her out of the seat.

"What is this?" she asked.

"It's too perfect of a night not to dance."

Before Paige could protest, he had taken her out to the sidewalk where other people were pairing up to dance. Paige loved dancing and, even though she wasn't particularly good at it or in the mood, it was hard to resist a man like Bryce Alexander.

It was so easy to get lost in him as he spun her around to the soft guitar. A million questions flooded through her, all of which she knew he would answer, but they couldn't pass her lips. She couldn't ruin this moment or what it could become.

"Bryce," she finally said, "I'm scared."

He swerved her away from another dancing couple. "Scared of what?" he asked. When she didn't answer, he pulled her close and led her over to their table. Instead of sitting across from her, he moved his chair to her side and took her hand in his. "Talk to me," he said.

"I…" Her voice failed and she reached for her water glass. "I've been thinking about what you said when we first got here. And, after spending more time with you, I think it might be something I want to pursue."

"But?"

Paige looked down at where their hands met. "But I'm scared of ruining what we already have. What if you're wrong and we don't work together? What if one of us becomes too invested? It would destroy everything."

Bryce reached up, taking his hat off and pushing his hair back before leaning closer. "Paige, I don't want to make you uncomfortable. God knows, that's not why I brought it up in the first place." He paused, like he was trying to think of the right words. "And I don't want you to think I'm pressuring you. But I can promise you that there is nothing that can affect us. I don't know why you're so worried when what we already have, our friendship, is magical. Why not see if there are fireworks when we try something...more?"

The way he said it, tilting his head down so that she had to see his grinning face, made her concerns feel trivial. He was right. Nothing could tear them apart, not even a one-night experiment. And she wanted it. Paige truly wanted Bryce, and with a smile, she nodded, confirming, if only to herself, that she would be spending the night in his room.

"Really?" Bryce closed the small space between them, stopping a breath away from her. Paige gasped, but she didn't move away. He was giving her a chance, just one opportunity to tell him no or to push him away. And she didn't. She couldn't.

"Yes." Paige reached up, pulling him to her. This time she didn't hold back and neither did he. It was a trial run like last time, and the fear of rejection or turning back was nowhere to be found. She couldn't wait to get home, to see what else Bryce had in store. Would he be soft and tender with her? Or would he be rough and take her as soon as the door was closed?

More importantly, will it change my mind about him or make things worse? Paige couldn't allow that thought. She slid her fingers up into Bryce's hair and pulled him closer, opening her mouth to invite him in. It was her darkest fantasy, one that she'd worked hard to suppress. Bryce would always be the unattainable, the one who wasn't right for one reason or another. But, for a few breathless moments, he was hers, and that was what mattered.

"Pardon me." The waiter was back. The pair jumped apart, a blush heating Paige's face and Bryce chuckling nervously. The waiter was unfazed and only smiled politely as he set their orders before them.

Paige stared down at the meal but, as delicious as it smelled, Paige's appetite was gone. She shared a look with Bryce, who reached out to stop the waiter.

"Could we get a couple of to-go boxes, please?"

Chapter Ten

July 18

Paige sucked in a deep breath while the phone rang in her ear. She wished she had some gum or something to do with her hands. Anything would be better than pacing the sea-green rug in Bryce's bathroom. It was a small space, and she was starting to feel dizzy, but the feeling of the shag under her bare feet was calming in its own way.

The ringing stopped mid-tone and there was a faint static noise as he picked up.

"Hello?" Levi's voice sounded groggy, and Paige knew that she'd woken him up.

"Hey, Levi," she said, trying her best to sound chipper as she cringed. "I'm sorry for calling so early." Her watch told her that it was nearly noon.

"It's no problem," he said after clearing his throat. "I should probably be getting up anyway. I had a late one last night. How's the vacation going?"

"Great," was all that she could say. "It's very hot out." Paige pressed the heel of her hand to her forehead, her pacing slowing only slightly. "Listen... I know that I'm a day early, but I thought I'd go ahead and let you know my decision about your offer."

"Okay," he said after a few beats of silence. "Don't leave me hanging, Paige."

"I, um, I don't think I'll be able to take it," she said, each word like needles jamming in her throat. "It's not that I don't appreciate it, and I'm beyond honored that you would even ask, but there's a lot of pressure, and I don't think that I'm in the right state of mind to create the way the job would demand and —"

"Paige," Levi said, his voice low and soft, "take a breath for me, okay? If you think I'm going to be mad, you're wrong. Do I think you're underestimating yourself? Absolutely. But I'm not going to browbeat you into this."

"Thank you," she said. She couldn't begin to describe the relief that washed over her, like she'd been carrying a backpack full of rocks the past week and was finally able to drop it. She drew in a deep breath and let it out completely. "For what it's worth, I'm sorry."

"Don't apologize. And just so you know, if I get another easel open in the future, you'll be the first person I call. Don't feel obligated, but don't forget that you have options."

"I might take you up on that one day," she said, smiling easily.

"Hey, while I've got you on the line, do you know when you'll be back in town? There's something else I want to talk to you about, something that has nothing to do with the gallery."

"I'll be back by the end of the month," Paige told him. She put him on speaker and set the phone down on the counter while she brushed out her hair.

"If you're interested, we can talk about it over dinner?" He'd phrased it as a question.

Paige stopped moving. She had the distinct feeling that he wasn't asking her to catch up as friends. Paige picked up the phone, glancing over at the closed door as she took it off speaker. She and Bryce were separated by a thin piece of wood and nothing more.

"I'll let you know as soon as I get back," she said. "We can talk about it then."

"I'll be looking forward to it," Levi said. "I'll talk to you later, Paige."

"Bye." A short beep sounded as he hung up and Paige slumped down onto the rug. Why was it that when she tried to picture herself on a date with Levi, she could only see herself with Bryce? He'd gotten into her head since she'd arrived in Florida. And, after last night, she was utterly lost to him.

She could still feel his hands on her, his fingers sliding under her clothes, exploring with a strange mix of curiosity and eagerness. The way his lips slid along her body, finding secrets that even she had been unaware of, wouldn't be easy to forget once they were out of Miami. How was she going to face him in the light of day without turning beet-red?

Paige growled in frustration and shoved her fingers into her half-tangled hair. Her phone dinged and a stream of incoming messages from Bryce flooded the screen. They were all photos, the ones that he had taken the day before. There were pictures of her impromptu art, of the two of them together and some of her on her own. She hadn't realized he'd taken so many, or that he'd taken photos while she was painting. Paige stared down at her own face. She looked...happy. Truly happy.

Paige pulled the door open, surprised at the empty room that greeted her. She picked up her shoes and hat before sneaking back to her own room. She couldn't very well go into the living room wearing the same dress as the night before. She tossed everything into the corner and threw on a tank top and a pair of polka dot pajama shorts.

"Good morning, sunshine," Jade chirped from the kitchen as Paige shuffled over to the couch. "How's my girl?"

Jade had no idea what had happened last night as she slept. Paige had to clear her throat a couple of times before she could speak without her voice cracking.

"Tired," she said, settling on the couch. Normally, she would have fallen face-first into the cushions, but panic was keeping her upright. What would Jade think if she found out? It was something Paige had already considered, but the reality hadn't set in.

One thing was certain—Jade could never know. She hoped that Bryce wouldn't tell Spencer. Given the hostility between them, she doubted they would spend their time gossiping about girls.

"What would you do without me?" Jade asked, bringing a warm mug of raspberry tea to Paige.

"I know what I would do without Spencer," Paige assured her with a forced grin. "I would marry you." She took a drink and breathed deeply. Her head began to clear, and her smile became more real.

"So, how was last night?" Jade asked.

Paige nearly choked on her drink. There was a slight flash of guilt as she remembered the night before. "It was nice. I got to paint." She swirled the contents of her mug. "I'm sorry we stayed out late."

"I don't remember y'all coming in. Spencer was frustrated this morning," Jade told her. "And before you say anything, he knows that Bryce is grown, but he's worried sick about him." Their conversation drew to a halt when both of their phones pinged at the same time. In unison, they reached for their devices and saw that a video had been sent from Clint's number.

"I swear, if this is another prank on Kindall…" Paige unlocked her phone.

"If he keeps messing with her and sending the videos to everyone on his contact list, she's going to leave him." Jade tapped her own screen to play the video.

Paige watched as Clint and Kindall stood in front of a Ferris wheel. She'd almost forgotten about the festival. It had been postponed that year due to weather, but the Donnes were set to have it. Jade gasped, but Paige's eyes were glued to the screen. In the video, it was nighttime and the lights from the attraction and lanterns were enough for her to see Clint drop to one knee.

"I can't believe he didn't tell us!" Jade said as Kindall jumped up in excitement and threw her arms around Clint's neck. "I need to call him!"

"I'll go tell the boys," Paige volunteered, any tiredness long gone. "Where are they?"

"Down at the beach," Jade said, pressing her phone to her ear.

Paige ran through the sliding glass door, ignoring the fact that she was in her pajamas, and hopped down the patio steps two at a time. She spotted them near the fire pit, both of them seated in the chairs that she and Bryce had occupied only nights ago.

She slowed when she heard them talking. It sounded serious. She was starting to back away, thinking she could tell them when they came inside, when she heard her name.

"Paige has been good for you, at least," Spencer said.

"What do you mean by that?" Bryce leaned back in the chair.

It would be best if she left. Just because they were talking about her didn't give her the right to listen in. But their backs were turned, and it was so easy to crouch out of sight behind the weathered fence.

"Well, you managed to stay out late last night without incident. And you've gone out with Paige before without problems." He paused. "Is there something going on with you two?"

Paige bit her lip. Whatever Bryce said next would decide how and where she spent the rest of her vacation. She was already thinking about flights to New York that could leave within the next couple of hours.

"I'm comfortable around her," Bryce said with a shrug. "She doesn't come with any pressure. It's like I can be myself with her."

"I'm sorry that you don't feel that way around me." Spencer adjusted in his seat and Paige crouched farther down. "I know I put a lot of pressure on you, and it's not fair. But, Bryce, that's the only way to learn responsibility." When Bryce didn't respond, he continued, "I'm under pressure, too, so I *do* understand how you feel. I'm so scared that I'm not going to be a good father."

The quiet that followed made it very clear that Spencer was opening himself up to Bryce. There was so much gravity in that one sentence, and Paige knew that none of it was meant for her ears. But she couldn't move. She wanted to be there in case something happened, and she needed to intervene. What if they started arguing again? At least, that's what she asked herself as she leaned closer, whether or not she believed it.

"Spence, don't be like that," Bryce said. "You know you're going to be great at this, the same way you're great at everything else."

"I'm worried that I won't be as good as our father," Spencer clarified. "I mean, he ran the company during some of its most successful years and still made time for us. He'd take us to the movies and help us with our homework. I don't think he ever missed a single game we played in. I don't know how to do any of that and have time for work." He sighed. "I know how crazy it sounds, but I need you to understand that you're not alone. We're all dealing with crap, and we'll never get through it all if we're not there for each other."

"I appreciate you trying to relate to me," Bryce said, "but I don't see it. You're not going to be like Dad, and no one is expecting you to. You're your own person, Spencer, and you're going to be an amazing father. Yes, you're a workaholic, but you're also great at prioritizing, and that kid is going to be your priority number one."

"And what if I lose focus?" Spencer prompted. "There's so much that could go wrong."

"You might every now and then, but Jade will only let you stray so far." Bryce turned more to face his brother. "And you'll have me there, too. Whenever you start to slack, cool Uncle Bryce will be there to swoop in and save the day. All you'll need to do is call me. But, could you please stop practicing your parenting skills on me?" What might have been a jab a few days ago was now a joke.

"I'll try my best," Spencer said, clapping a hand on his shoulder. "When did you grow up enough to start giving me advice?"

Paige smiled. Whatever had happened between them, she was glad to see that they could put it aside long enough to be there for each other. And Spencer had a point about Bryce's maturity. That had taken Paige by surprise as well, especially when Bryce had been the one scared of a baby niece or nephew only days ago. The brothers leaned back in their chairs and Paige suddenly remembered why she had come out there in the first place.

She stood, shaking the sand from her robe and marching over to them. "Y'all should probably come inside," she told them. "Jade has some news for you."

"What kind of news?" Spencer asked, jumping to his feet. "Good news?"

"You'll have to go ask her yourself." She smiled as he took off, then noticed that she'd been left alone with Bryce. He was staring at her, not making any move to follow Spencer. His hair was slicked back with drying seawater, and he had a towel draped over his bare shoulders.

Paige focused on the sand beneath her feet. "Don't you want to know what the fuss is about?"

"I'm sure someone will tell me sooner or later," Bryce said with a shrug. "To tell you the truth, I'm more interested in how your talk with Levi went."

"Don't pretend like you weren't listening in," Paige said. "The doors around here aren't thick." When she looked up at him, Bryce was genuinely affronted.

"I woke up when you got up. I heard you pacing around the bathroom and saying hi to Levi, so I figured I'd give you some privacy." He moved closer and Paige could feel herself trying to lean away. "Unlike you, I don't like to listen in on others' conversations unless invited."

Paige swallowed hard and smiled nervously. "I'm really sorry about that."

"I don't care," Bryce said. "Like I told you, I want to know how your phone call went."

"I turned down the job. It was like you said, between the pressure and not knowing if he was also searching for a relationship, it wasn't a smart move for me."

"Does this mean you're not interested in anything he has to offer?"

"I wouldn't say that," Paige laughed. "Why are you so curious? I thought this was casual."

"It is," Bryce said. "As long as you want it to be." Something in his tone set her on edge. It was dangerous enough, even though they'd only spent one night together. It was all so vivid in her mind—the way he'd whispered in her ear as he held her, comforting her and guiding her through the night, showing her how amazing he could make her feel.

She knew that he would notice, but Paige couldn't resist looking him up and down. He was magnificent, tall and lean and tanned, and Paige had the urge to reach out and touch him. The guilt and hesitation left. Standing there with Bryce felt right. The night before, when his arms had been around her, when his mouth had been against hers, hot and needy, it had felt right.

She wanted more of those kisses and days on the town with Bryce.

"Listen," Paige said, "about last night —"

"You don't have to worry about anything," he said quickly. "I know better than to say anything to Spencer. I don't think Jade would mind, but big brother wouldn't be too happy with our…activities." He leaned over, nipping at Paige's ear. "Then there's us, friends the morning after. Nothing has to change."

And there was the lie. Everything had changed, at least for Paige. They would finish out their vacation together, but after that they would start to drift. They wouldn't call or text to check in on each other anymore, and Paige would miss that. And it would be Paige's decision. She knew what Bryce was like and how he would treat her, and it had made her fall for him more.

"Let's head back in," Bryce said. "I'm curious about Jade's news." He scooted around her, heading up the worn steps to the house.

Paige didn't want to move. She wanted to stand right there and turn back time. She wanted to speak up and tell him how much he meant to her and how much she wanted him to kiss her again. She wanted to admit that she'd made a mistake and that *she* was the one becoming too involved. But she couldn't. Instead, Paige followed after Bryce with a brand-new weight on her chest.

Chapter Eleven

July 21

Paige wrapped a towel over her sparkly purple bikini. It had been years since she'd snorkeled, but being back under the clear blue Miami water had brought all those memories back. The coral was vibrant and equally colorful fish darted in and out of the openings, some of them brushing over Paige's skin as they swam past.

And right there next to her was Bryce—handsome, confusing, irritating Bryce. To his credit, he'd been very well behaved as far as the parties went since their arrival. And, since he'd gotten closer to Paige, she'd noticed that his flirtatious ways toward other women had cooled down. Now, his one-liners and innuendo were reserved only for her.

"How long were we swimming?" Paige asked as she stacked her gear next to one of the lounge chairs.

Bryce checked his watch. "About an hour," he said. "It didn't feel like it, though."

"No, it didn't."

"Are you feeling all right?" Bryce asked. "Do you need anything?"

Paige's breaths were coming out sharp and fast. "Oh, I'm okay," she said. "It's been a while since I swam that much. I guess I'm not as in-shape as I used to be." She waded to the surf where her towel waited. Taking off all the gear allowed the sun to warm her damp skin.

"You look fine to me," Bryce said, his eyes dropping down her figure.

"Cut it out," Paige said, only half joking. Jade and Spencer were lost in their own conversation, but she was paranoid that they would overhear. It had been bad enough having to sneak in and out of Bryce's room every night, but it was well worth it.

"So," Jade said, once they'd settled down into the sand, "what else do you want to do today?"

"More of the usual," Bryce said. All eyes turned to him. "Okay, I know that sounded sarcastic, but I'm serious. I think a day at the beach and grilling out would be nice. I mean, we've already had a good start, right?"

"You have to be careful," Spencer reminded Jade. "You can't be outside for long, and I don't want us doing anything too rough. Snorkeling was already pushing it, in my opinion."

"I did my research and it's perfectly fine for me to snorkel. Why don't we let Paige pick what we do next? She's been quiet this week."

"Me?" Paige nearly jumped out of her skin. "I'm not being quiet. I've been focused on having fun."

"Then let's have some fun," Bryce said with a smile that was just for her. "What do you wanna do?"

She thought about what they used to do in high school. Spencer would immediately turn down volleyball or dodgeball. She thought about the water guns she'd noticed in the shed the other day, but that made her think of laser tag with Bryce. Not to mention it would probably be too intense for Spencer's liking. Then, it hit her. Running the towel over her pink-striped hair one last time, Paige stood.

"I propose a sand art competition," she said, hands fisted on her hips.

"Isn't that on the nose for you?" Jade asked.

"And wouldn't you have an unfair advantage over us?" Spencer piped in.

"I'll be the judge," Paige said, brushing sand from her legs. She led them up to the shed where they loaded up on plastic pails and shovels. Bryce and Spencer were already trash talking each other while Jade discussed her ideas with Paige. She tried her best to pay attention to Jade's words, but all she could focus on was the small bump under Jade's blue and gray bathing suit.

The boys raced each other to the beach, Paige shouting after them, "Anyone starting before I say will be disqualified!"

The contest was much more heated than Paige had anticipated, with the Alexanders' competitive sides shining brightly. Bryce would go to get a bucket of water only to 'accidentally' trip over Spencer's castle. In turn, Spencer would throw shells like ninja stars at Bryce's mermaid statue and knock her arms and head off.

In the end, Jade was the obvious winner. Her castle was nothing spectacular, but Bryce's sculpture was a misshapen blob and Spencer's was a pile of sand. At least Paige could tell what Jade had made. Even when the contest was called, Bryce and Spencer continued to work in vain on their failed projects while the women sat under their umbrellas.

"It looks like they're doing better," Jade said. "Whatever you're doing, it's working. Bryce likes you, you know. He tried his best to get Spencer to set you two up forever ago."

"What? When was that?" He'd never expressed any interest in Paige until recently, right?

"It was a bit after the wedding," Jade said with a giggle. "I think it was the week after we got back from our honeymoon. But don't worry. Spencer made it clear that you were off limits. I think he's past it anyway, so you have nothing to worry about."

Paige laughed along with Jade, but a pit had opened in her stomach. All the flirtations that she'd written off, all the times she'd wondered what might have happened between them if she'd acted on her crush… But that was all it was, a crush. And what Jade had told her changed nothing.

"Who is that?" Bryce asked, pointing toward the house to where a burgundy Jeep Wrangler was parking too close to the patio. Spencer stood, squinting up at the car on top of the hill.

"I have no idea," Jade said, almost to herself.

Paige's jaw nearly hit the ground when Levi Gould stepped out of the driver's seat. He shut the door and waved down to them on the beach. All eyes turned to Paige, as though she could explain the newcomer. She stumbled to her feet, a challenge with the sand and her nerves, and ran up the steps to the lawn.

"You're a hard woman to find, Miss Montgomery," he said with a dazzling smile. "What on earth have you done to your hair?"

Paige reached up, combing her hair out so that he could see the full style. "Don't you love it?" she asked.

"It's different," he said carefully. "Not something I was thinking I'd see when I got here, but I guess it's good to try new things." He wrapped an arm around her in a small hug.

"What are you doing here?" She'd never seen him like that before, in knee-length shorts and a black T-shirt, though he still wore his combat boots, despite the heat. Levi was the type to layer his clothes, and she noted that he'd hidden a lot with that strategy. Arms corded with muscle emerged from his sleeves and the shirt stretched tight over his chest.

"I had to talk to you and I didn't think a phone call would suffice. Shall we?"

Paige led him back down to the sand where he nodded to the curious group gathered on the beach.

"Levi, you know Jade," Paige said. "And you've met Spencer. This is his brother, Bryce."

"Ah, the famous Bryce Alexander," Levi said. "The man Paige gives her best work away to."

Bryce stepped forward and shook his hand, but the look in his eyes wasn't friendly. Glancing at Levi, she saw he shared the hostility. *It's your imagination,* she told herself. They had only just met, so there was no way they could hate each other from the start.

"I'm sorry to drop in so unexpectedly," Levi said, addressing Jade and Spencer. "You wouldn't mind if I borrowed Paige for a few minutes, would you?"

Grabbing her towel, Paige followed Levi a way down the beach. She could see other people on their own private sections of beach, but the Alexanders' stretch was large enough to allow some privacy. Once they were far enough away to not be overheard, Levi stopped and turned to face Paige.

"I wanted you to know that I turned down the offer for your easel." Levi crossed his arms and looked down at her. "It's open if you want it."

"Levi, we talked about this," Paige said. She eased herself down onto the sand. "I told you that I don't feel ready, and you promised not to push. "

"That's true, but I've been thinking about it. I think I've confused you with my mixed signals, so I'm here to tell you, in person, exactly what I want. No more games or dancing around it." Levi knelt next to her. "Paige, you are more talented than most people ever dream of becoming, but you know that's not the entire reason I want you at my studio."

"I think so," Paige said. "But I'd like to hear it from you."

"Fine. I like you, and I have for a very long time. Since the beginning, I think. Getting to work close to you, to know that you're only a short drive away, is something I've had the pleasure of experiencing while we were getting ready for our show, and I don't want to lose that."

"You wanted me to be nearby? You could have told me that from the beginning," Paige said.

"But it's not only that," Levi brushed his braids over his shoulder and leaned in closer. "I'm doing this wrong. You're distracted out here and, with me showing up out of the blue, you can't take me seriously. Why don't you let me take you to that dinner I offered?"

"Levi..." Paige didn't know what to say to him anymore. She glanced over her shoulder, her eyes automatically drifting to Bryce.

"I know how this looks, and your hesitation is understandable. I'm a tenacious guy, and I know what I want. I don't think I gave you enough time to consider my offer, so give me one more chance to convince you that this is the right move." He tipped her head toward him with a finger. "Give me this last chance to convince you to stay with me, Paige."

Chills prickled up and down Paige's arm. It *was* about more than the job.

"Tonight," Paige said with a smile, "you get one chance to see where this takes us. Make it count, Gould." She'd never been great at flirting, but she gave her best impression of a coy smile. Whatever she did seemed to work, because Levi let out a soft laugh.

"Wonderful," he said as he stood up. "I'll be by at seven to pick you up."

Paige's smile widened and she nodded as Levi walked away, that strange fluttering returning to her chest. *Funny, the last time that happened was with Bryce.* But what Bryce offered was fleeting. Levi showing up could be the thing that helped her move away from Bryce and their temporary arrangement. She could forget about what Jade had inadvertently brought up. Why stress over off-limits Bryce when Levi was right there?

"What was all that about?" Bryce asked, making her jump.

"Levi wanted to tell me that the offer stands," Paige said with a shrug.

"He flew all the way to Miami and tracked you down for something he could have told you over the phone?" he asked with a raised brow. "Come on, Paige. You can do better than that."

"There was more," she started, choosing her words, "but he's going to tell me the rest tonight over dinner." She didn't know why she was keeping it from him. Whatever it was between her and Bryce was casual, something they could call off at any time. But that all felt wrong to her.

Bryce crossed his arms, and she glanced up long enough to see the flash of disappointment in his eyes before he controlled his features.

"Don't let him pressure you, Paige," Bryce said. "You told him no for a reason. I don't want to see you pushed into something you don't want to make someone else happy."

"Thanks for looking out for me," she said sincerely. "I promise I won't let him get to me if he brings up the job."

Bryce nodded and started to leave. "Paige," he said over his shoulder, "do you think you'll come to my room tonight?"

Paige stood, her thumbnail between her teeth. She already knew that she didn't want the job at Levi's studio, but she was undecided about the man himself. Dinner, for her, was a test to see if there were earnest feelings for Levi. She was attracted to him—only an idiot wouldn't be. It would feel dishonest to lead Levi on for a few hours then spend the night next to Bryce. And Paige wasn't that kind of person.

"I'm not sure," she said as honestly as she could. Levi might not be her first choice, but he was safer, and she owed him a chance. Bryce nodded his understanding and left her there. Over time, Paige would be able to get over her infatuation with Bryce

Alexander. She would have to—and Levi would only help.

Chapter Twelve

"It's just dinner," Paige whispered to herself, removing the curling iron from a lock of hair. "You've done this before." *But not with Levi,* she finished in her head. *And not when you were hooked on Bryce.*

"I'm not hooked," she argued with the mirror. It was a stupid thing to do out loud, but it soothed her nerves. She didn't consider herself another one of Bryce's conquests, but it was probably common for him to have a summer fling every year. He was young, handsome and rich. He had a future ahead of him, even if it was unsteady at the moment, and he could have any woman that he wanted. Paige was...convenient. That was a word that wouldn't destroy her completely.

She unplugged the curling iron and leaned against the bathroom counter. Unlike the other women he surrounded himself with, Paige didn't care about his family or his bank account. She liked the vulnerable parts about him, the ones that he locked away and only showed glimpses of to her. She liked how he made her feel seen and inspired. He'd been wrapped up in the glamour that came with his surname, but she couldn't hold that against him.

There were two sides to every coin, and she'd seen how he'd used the fame as a mask. His family was an excuse that he used to pretend to be someone he wasn't. And, worst of all, people bought it. The tabloids loved to talk about the wayward Alexander and how he acted out. But, despite the womanizing, Paige nearly had him figured out. The only problem was that, in the process, she'd started falling in love with him.

Whether it had started with the first kiss a year before or during one of their nightly exploits, she was in deep and needed to back away. Paige checked herself one last time in the mirror, adjusting her wavy hair and smoothing down her emerald-green sequined dress. She had chosen a pair of flashing silver heels to go with it. She knew Levi and he would settle for nothing less than the best restaurant he could find, so it would pay to dress up.

"You're off already?" Jade asked as Paige entered the living room.

"Not yet," she told her. "He won't be here for another ten minutes." Unless he showed up earlier, which Levi had a tendency to do. "What do you think?" She spun, the skirt fluttering around her knees.

"Very nice," Jade said. "Levi doesn't stand a chance."

Paige looked around the room and, though Spencer was missing, Bryce was sitting at the kitchen bar with his shoulders hunched as he scrolled on his phone. Wasn't he even going to sneak a glance her way? It occurred to Paige that part of her dressing up might have been to get Bryce's attention, which only made her chest tighten.

"I think I heard a car," she lied, grabbing her wrap and bag from the couch. "Don't wait up." And, without a look back to see if anyone had acknowledged her, Paige left.

She knew why it bothered her, and she hated herself for it. She shouldn't *want* Bryce's attention in the first place, least of all that night. It was supposed to be about Levi and what he wanted from her. She would hear him out and give him his chance. And, if he brought up the job again, at least she wouldn't be thinking about Bryce.

It was only a few minutes later that Levi's bright red Wrangler pulled into the drive and stopped beside her.

"Somebody's ready for a hot date," he said out the open passenger window. "Who are you all dressed up for?"

"I might have someone in mind," Paige said, though she wasn't sure if she meant Levi or Bryce.

On the way to the restaurant, which he still wouldn't divulge to her, Levi caught Paige up on the happenings in New York. His studio had been featured in several magazines from the showing, and a picture of the pair of them had made it into most of the articles.

"I took a screenshot to send to you, but I didn't want to disrupt your vacation," he told her.

"Sending a picture would have been a disruption, but flying down and taking me to dinner is perfectly acceptable?"

"Any excuse to take you out is acceptable," Levi said.

They pulled up to a restaurant called Caine's, a new building that she'd never heard of before, though it was a few miles from where she was staying. Levi handed his keys to the valet and took her arm. He was strong and handsome and wearing that leather jacket that she loved so much. His scarf was black with threads of gold, and he wore dark jeans with his combat boots. Even when going to a five-star restaurant, he couldn't be bothered to dress up.

Eyes watched them from every direction as they were led to a candle-lit table in the back, and Paige was proud to be by his side. She kept the smile on her face as they sat down, Levi pulling her chair out, and they were handed their menus. Paige couldn't shake the feeling that something didn't feel right.

"You've been working." Levi wasn't asking a question.

"How would you know?" Paige asked. She hadn't mentioned anything about it. She'd been more than happy to let Levi carry the conversation so far.

"You have graphite on your hand," he told her, pointing to the side of her wrist. He was right. Paige grabbed a napkin and tried her best to scrape away the shiny markings that had made it through her shower. "Allow me," Levi said. He took his own napkin and dipped it into his water glass, gently taking her hand in his and wiping the marks away.

"Thank you," Paige said as the waiter arrived and took their orders. As soon as he left, Levi turned his attention to Paige again.

"Tell me about your sketches," he said, taking a sip of water. "I know it's not your usual medium of choice."

Paige was relieved that they could start dinner with something easy for her to talk about. She told him about her morning drawings, the trip to Little Havana where she'd tried spray painting and about the sculpture she'd failed to finish or even really start. It was a rust-colored clump sitting on a pile of newspaper in her room. The only thing she glossed over was Bryce.

"It's a good thing to get out of your comfort zone, especially when you're stuck," he said. "Now, Paige, I need you to tell me why you're in Miami."

Paige blinked a few times, trying to think of the best way to answer. "We're all here for a vacation," she told him. "And I could use some inspiration. I think I'm trying to find my next steps. I don't know what I'm supposed to be doing and, for some reason, I think I'm going to find it here."

"I wouldn't think someone such as yourself would ever lack inspiration."

"It happens. Everyone thinks that an artist is always free to express themselves, but I've been told what to paint my whole life. I love it, but I never feel like I'm putting myself onto the canvas." She laughed. "I don't know why I'm telling you all of this. You know exactly what I'm talking about."

"I might be one of the few people in your life who truly understands," Levi agreed. "Here's what I think, based on the little I've seen so far. I think you've found that inspiration you needed, and you're afraid you'll lose it if you leave this place. At the same time, you're also afraid to tie yourself down. Am I right?"

"You're right," Paige said. "I'm trying to find something real here, something that I can hold on to, so I'm clinging to the city for now and enjoying it while it lasts." She thought about Bryce and how he made her feel. "Levi, I've felt something here that I've never felt before."

"Look around you, Paige. This isn't real. You're living in a place where people go to escape their lives."

He ran a hand back through his braids. "Whatever you've found here won't last, no matter how long you stay. What I'm offering you? That's real. New York can be just as inspiring if you find the right people and places."

Levi reached across the table for her hand, rubbing his thumb over her knuckles. "I don't want to lose you to some fantasy. That's why I'm here. This career can be tricky. Finding work can get hard sometimes. You're on top now, Paige, but it might not last forever. What I want for you is the chance to work at your own pace without having to worry about money. Why take risks by going at it by yourself?"

"So you want me to commit to a location, just not here? Why are you trying to make this about work again?" Paige asked with minor annoyance. She'd known it would come up, but she hadn't wanted it to happen so soon. Wasn't this supposed to be a date?

"It's not all about work." Levi looked up at her. "I'm not trying to sell you on the job being good for you. I would be good for you, too." He let go of her hand long enough to move his chair around the table. It was the same thing Bryce had done at Slice of Lime, and Paige was having serious déjà vu. "I want you in my studio because of your talent." He reached up and touched her cheek. "I want you close to me for more amorous reasons. And, before you let the temporary magic of this town and the Alexanders get to you, think about what you'll leave behind."

Paige was ready. She let her eyes shut as their lips met, a small breath disappearing between them. Levi was everything she could ever want and, as his mouth moved with hers, she knew that he would be perfect for her and would keep her content. But that was it. As wonderful as Levi was, the sparks that she'd felt with Bryce simply weren't there. Levi was slow and careful with her, but she didn't feel the same life and passion that she did with Bryce.

Levi pulled back. "Are you okay?" he asked, holding her face in his hand.

"Yes," she said breathlessly. "I'm...confused."

"I didn't come on too strong, did I?"

"No, I guess I have a lot to think about," She laughed, raising her hand to cover his. She'd need to sleep on it, but she was beginning to doubt that she could be truly happy with Levi. Would it be fair to him if she tried?

"How about we don't bring it up for the rest of the night?" Levi suggested. "The job or what just happened... You can take tonight to think it over, and we'll discuss it when you're ready. I'm not interested in scaring you away."

Paige nodded her agreement. They spent the rest of dinner reminiscing about their college years and swapping stories about their travels. Though Levi did almost bring up the job again, he caught himself and steered away from the topic.

After dinner, Levi returned Paige to the beach house, going so far as to walk her to the front door. "We should do this again before I leave," he said. His smile was so dazzling and even, not like Bryce's that turned up higher on his right side.

"I feel like I'm in high school again, being dropped off at my parents' house," she said, mostly to fill the space and move away from thoughts of Bryce. "My dad might be waiting up inside to lecture me about staying out so late."

"The only difference here is" — Levi looked down at his Rolex — "you're home after midnight and there's no one waiting to ground you for it." He moved closer. "You don't have to go in yet, Cinderella. We could go anywhere you want."

It was tempting. She knew that the household would likely be asleep by that time. The windows were all dark. Would anyone notice if she didn't come home that night? *Bryce would.* Levi was beautiful and perfect and clearly into her. And she didn't want to spend the night with him. Was she an idiot? *Maybe,* Paige mused, *romantic feelings will follow if I get farther from Bryce.*

"I should probably get to bed," she said. "But, if you want, you could come over tomorrow. I'm not sure what the plan is or if we have one yet, but you're more than welcome."

"I might take you up on that," he said. "May I kiss you goodnight, Paige?"

It was so sweet that she could have melted on the spot. He took both of her hands in his and leaned down to plant a chaste kiss on her lips. Again, so sweet that she nearly gagged. Levi would make someone very happy someday, but could it be her? They made a terrific couple on paper, if that photo circulating the art magazines was anything to go by. And they were both artists who had been friends for years and who understood each other. Maybe she wasn't giving Levi a fair chance. It had only been one dinner.

Levi bade her a goodnight and pulled away once she'd unlocked and opened the door. *He's a great guy,* she thought. When she closed the door behind her, a flickering light caught her attention. Bryce was sitting in one of the living room chairs, scrolling through his phone, as he had been before she left.

Paige turned to lock the door, wondering what she should say to him or if she should say anything, when she noticed the windowpane. There was a clear view to the front porch and, with the outside light on, anyone in the living room would be able to see anything happening at the door.

"You were out late," Bryce said casually.

"Yes, I was." Paige locked the door and turned to face him. "I said I would be before I left."

"Did you at least have a good time?" He continued to stare down at his phone.

"I did. Why do you care?"

"I don't."

"Liar," Paige said. "You wouldn't be out here if that were true. Don't tell me you're jealous."

"He seems pushy to me," Bryce said. "I had to make sure you were all right."

"He was perfectly considerate," she defended. "And you don't get any say in this. As per our deal, I'm allowed to date whomever I want."

"I don't get any say?" He looked over at her, the hurt in his eyes reflected in the light from his screen.

"That's right. You remember our terms." She tried to rush past Bryce to the stairs. "I'm not doing this tonight."

Bryce beat her to the steps, reaching for her arm and holding her in place with the slight touch. "Paige," was all he said.

"If you have something to tell me, get on with it. Otherwise, let me go to my room."

Bryce stared at her, his hand burning against her skin. Finally, he released her and stepped away.

"You wouldn't believe me if I did," he said. "But I don't like what's happening with Levi, and nothing you do can stop me from saying so." He crossed the living room and headed out to the patio, slamming the door behind him.

They had made their agreement, and that included the freedom to see other people. Bryce was probably getting obsessive and upset because someone else was playing with his toy, because that was all that she was to him. That was all she could ever be. Paige dashed to her room before she could do something she would regret.

Chapter Thirteen

July 22

Bryce was not going to get to her. Paige was unsure about a lot in her life, but that was one thing she could be absolute about. Tossing and turning all night, thinking of nothing but Bryce, she'd managed to convince herself that he would never be right for her. She'd seen how he was with women. He was a serial romantic, always on the hunt for his next girlfriend who wouldn't last a week. And that was fine if it was what he wanted to do, but Paige didn't have the time for it.

She'd let herself live out the fantasy, and she couldn't be the savior who turned him around. Thinking about his kisses and the way he touched her made her skin tingle, but it wasn't real. There was nothing that Paige had to set her apart from the dozens of models Bryce had been with. It wasn't worth her time to try and be more than Bryce's summer fling.

He was too young for her, which was a point she'd clung to like a life preserver, because that's what it was. Even if she could justify every other excuse, Bryce's age and proximity to Jade were enough to make her start distancing herself.

Paige pulled a black sundress over her pink bikini and vowed that she wouldn't let Bryce in anymore. She wouldn't be sneaking into his room, no matter what he tried to do or say. She would enjoy the rest of her time in Miami without having to worry about him.

And you can devote a little more time to Levi, she reminded herself. He would be with them that night, and she would try her best to put on what charm she could muster. They were heading down to the marina where Spencer had rented a yacht for the night. It had been his idea to get them out of the house while doing something familiar.

For Paige, it was also nostalgic. She remembered the first time she'd gone on a yacht with Jade and the Alexander boys. It had been around the time that Jade and Spencer had been falling back in love and getting used to the idea of marriage. It was also the first time she'd officially met Bryce.

They had clicked instantly, playing in the water and flirting, though Paige had thought it was all in good fun. To her, it had been a way to poke fun at the lovesick couple they were stuck with. Over the course of a month, it had turned into something else, something that Paige was scared to admit to and something she couldn't imagine Bryce reciprocating.

Paige and Jade met up with the boys in the marina as they were readying the vessel for castoff. It was smaller than *The Absolution*, the Alexanders' yacht in New York, but this one sported a jacuzzi and observation deck. With the smooth LED light strips along the deck, it was clearly a party boat.

Levi stood at the step, his hands in the pockets of his black cargo pants. He wore a thin white shirt that, in the scant evening light, did nothing to hide his well-sculpted body. Jade nudged Paige, but she could only smile. It seemed that Jade approved of Levi.

He helped the women onto the yacht as Bryce began to reach for the mooring line. He paused, blatantly staring at Levi and Paige's entwined hands. When she noticed, Paige pulled her hand away from Levi, pretending that she had to help Jade over to a seat. She didn't know why she was trying to appease Bryce, but she could already feel the threads of tension forming between the three of them.

Spencer began to pull them out of the marina, and Bryce flipped a series of switches on the wall, causing more strands of lights to burst to life. The hot tub lit from the inside and began to bubble. Levi looked lost, like he wasn't sure what to do or where to sit, and Paige felt bad for him. These weren't his friends or people that he knew well. Paige's was the only familiar face, and she was distancing herself from him.

Paige stood up and suggested that she and Levi sit together on one of the padded couches near the tub. She wasn't going to let the fact that Bryce was there keep her from Levi anymore. After the night before, she didn't owe him anything. He'd already caused a rift between them by backing out of their deal.

It was getting darker, and though they were out in open water, she could see the lights of the bay and hear the sounds that came with it. There were a few smaller boats zooming across the water nearby, but the yacht kept a slow, leisurely pace.

The deck soon became quite awkward, and Paige would have liked an excuse to leave, but she stayed by Levi's side and stared at the horizon. The next time she risked a glance at Bryce, he was leaning back against the railing, his arms crossed as he looked everywhere but the couch. Finally, the yacht stopped and there was a quiet mechanical whir as the anchor was lowered. Spencer returned with a cooler while Bryce hopped down onto the swim platform, removing his T-shirt before diving into the water.

"Is it just me or is he moody tonight?" Levi asked. "I know it's not my place, but…"

"He's going through some stuff," Paige explained delicately. "Don't take it personally, okay?" *Even if it might be.*

"I'm sure you're right," Levi said, then lowered his voice so that only she could hear, "but he seems to hate me. Am I imagining that?"

Paige swallowed hard and shook her head. She had been hoping she could get away with her lies. Drinks were passed around as Spencer and Levi hit it off. As business owners, Paige could understand that they would have common ground, but their conversation didn't hold her interest. Jade was ignoring them, too, sitting by the hot tub with her legs dangling in the bubbles.

"Is anyone else getting into the water?" Bryce asked, climbing back on the platform. "Paige?"

"Oh, I don't think so," she said. "You go ahead and enjoy yourself."

"I can't," Bryce said, lifting himself onto the deck, "when I'm by myself." He had that look in his eye, the one that made Paige worried. It was the same one from the night at the arcade before he'd tried to annihilate her at laser tag.

"No," she said, her arms out in front of her as he marched over. "No, no, no!" She couldn't stop laughing, though. For that second, she forgot about the kiss and Levi and what her life was becoming. With next-to-no effort, Bryce scooped her up from the couch. Levi said something in protest, but she couldn't hear him.

"Jade is pregnant and everyone else is too big for me to lift like this," Bryce pointed out. "You made yourself an easy target."

"Bryce," Paige pleaded. "Bryce, don't you dare!" She began to struggle as Bryce passed the jacuzzi to get down to the swim platform. Tucked firmly against his strong chest, she knew that fighting was pointless, but it didn't stop her from flailing.

"Deep breath," he warned before releasing her, tossing her into the surprisingly cool water. It wasn't cold, but when it wrapped around her, it felt amazing. A sudden memory filled her mind, and she opened her eyes. It was dark under the surface, but she wasn't afraid.

It was four years earlier on *The Absolution,* and Bryce had dragged her under the water. It wasn't malicious, and when she'd been able to get her bearings, Bryce had already swum several yards away. She'd followed, ignoring Jade and Spencer behind her, and caught up to him quickly.

That was when it had started, if she was admitting it to herself. Their play fighting had brought them close, and that's when she'd noticed just how blue his eyes were, with those dark lashes around them. There were hidden freckles on his skin, something she'd never seen on Spencer. And his smile was crooked as he laughed, and it had captivated her.

It was easy to brush off seconds later. There were plenty of people taken aback by an attractive human being, right? It didn't have to mean anything. She'd dunked him back under the water and swum to the yacht as quickly as she could, only to discover Jade and Spencer in their own embrace. It wasn't until later that she would make the mistake of getting to know Bryce and finding out that there was so much more to him than pretty eyes and kissable lips.

Paige broke the surface of the water, her lungs burning for air. Bryce was a couple of feet away, with that same smile and a new expression, one that was more determined, more intense and directed at her. This time, she could tell that he wasn't playing around.

"I was about to go under after you," he said. "Are you okay?"

"I wanted to scare you," Paige said. "You deserved it."

"I guess that makes us even now?" he asked quietly. "I'm sorry about how I acted last night. You didn't deserve that." He glanced up at the boat. "You're different around him, you know. You act like you're worried you'll be judged. It's not something everyone can see, but I do. It's why I don't trust him with you."

"He's a professional critic," Paige said with a shrug. "I want to put my best out there for him."

Bryce swam closer. "The Paige in front of me isn't her best," he whispered. "She's too busy trying to look like she has everything together. Paige, we have to talk about this. And I do mean talk as friends, not argue as whatever it is that we are now."

"I have some things together," Paige said weakly. The sun had almost set completely and most of the light came from the boat above them. "We've already talked enough. In case it wasn't clear, our arrangement is over. We're back to being friends, end of discussion. Levi's here now, and it wouldn't be fair to him."

"And this is fair to me? In case *I* wasn't clear, I don't want this to be some fling. I'm tired of pretending that what's happening here doesn't mean more to me."

"Then tell me what it means," Paige demanded. When Bryce pressed his lips together, she sighed. "Can't this wait until we get back to the house?"

"I've been waiting," Bryce said. He reached for her, his hand at the base of her neck. "I was patient because I thought I had more time. Then Levi showed up and—"

"And what?" Levi's voice came from above.

Paige felt like she'd been punched in the gut. She pulled away from Bryce, climbing onto the platform. Levi reached out to help her and Jade was staring at them, aware that something was happening and ready to diffuse a situation. Spencer was too busy messing with the sound system to notice.

"We weren't expecting company," Bryce said coolly behind her. "I'm having to adjust my plans to accommodate your…visit."

"If your plans aren't working out, maybe that's a sign that they aren't meant to," Levi said, matching his tone. Paige stared between them. She'd hoped they could all be adults about this, that Bryce would move on and she would be free to pursue Levi. He was the perfect choice, a person she could spend the rest of her life with.

Paige tugged her arm away from Levi, irritation and discomfort already marring the night.

"Well, I'm already soaked," she said to Jade. "Wanna go for a swim?" Paige tugged at the belt of her ruined chiffon dress and let it drop to the deck.

"Might as well." Jade shrugged. "I can't enjoy the hot tub right now."

"You couldn't pay me enough to get into that water," Levi said, though no one had asked. "I'll stick to the clean chemicals, thank you very much." He took his own shirt off and eased himself into the tub, gesturing for Paige to join him.

"I'll be all right," Paige said. She didn't want to be alone with him yet, and Spencer was already setting rules for a game of Jazzminton. "Are you sure you don't want to play?"

"There's all sorts of crap in the ocean," Levi told her. "I'm not taking that chance. And, for the record, I'm sorry if I made you uncomfortable. I don't know what Bryce's issues are, but he needs to stop projecting them onto you. And you're going to have to tell me what happened between you two."

"He's not—" Paige turned to look at the group on the water. "We've all got a lot to figure out. I'm trying to be there for my friends, and Bryce is one of them."

"There seems to be more than friendship to me." Paige could feel his eyes on her.

"Are you sure you'll be okay up here?" She wanted to pretend he hadn't asked those questions or seen through her so quickly, even if it was only for the night.

"Come on, Paige." Levi spread his arms out on the deck. "I'm in the lap of luxury. It won't be long until you get tired of that dirty water and want to join me." His eyes met hers. "I'm a patient man."

There was nothing else she could say. She knew that his statement had nothing to do with the ocean. She would have to get this mess figured out and fast. She would start by talking to Bryce, privately, tomorrow. She couldn't let this go on, especially if she wanted any future with Levi. Taking a deep breath, Paige ran and dove back into the water.

Chapter Fourteen

July 23

Jade wasn't doing well when Paige woke up. Morning sickness was not taking it easy on her, and she had been in bed all morning. The few times that Spencer had been down to get crackers or ginger ale, he'd updated Paige, assuring her that everything would be fine. It didn't console her much. Spencer was sweating bullets, and she was sure he'd developed a twitch in his left eye.

It would have been the perfect opportunity to talk to Bryce, but he hadn't left his room, and she hadn't heard a sound from him all morning. She'd stood outside his door, debating whether or not she should knock, before deciding against it. She knew why it was so hard for her. If she was the one to confront Bryce when it was just the two of them, she might give in. She might forget her worries and fears just seeing him.

Levi arrived later that afternoon and swore that Jade's sickness came from swimming in the ocean. Paige had stared at the TV, not bothering to point out that Jade had already improved and, if it had been something in the water, they all would have gotten sick.

Though it never rained, there were heavy clouds in the sky that seemed too threatening for outdoor activities. So, she and Levi had made their own fun, borrowing from the expansive collection of board games and video games in the hall closet. Spencer joined a few rounds and, when Bryce finally came into the living room, he seemed excited to play. Then he saw Levi.

"I just remembered I told Chris I would stop by today," Bryce said, already headed toward the patio door.

"Chris? As in our neighbor?" Spencer stood from the couch to face Bryce. "I thought you didn't like him. Didn't you say that he always stuck his nose in your business?"

Bryce shrugged. "I'm trying to make new friends," he said. "Maybe I just need to get to know him better. And, who knows? Maybe I'll find his endless questions endearing one day."

It was after they ordered pizza for dinner that Jade came downstairs looking tired. Paige couldn't stop thinking about the talk she would have to have and soon. The real trick would be getting away for a couple of minutes without garnering too much attention. She didn't know who Chris was, but if she could just get close and get Bryce's attention, she could fix everything.

Jade received a call from her mother halfway through dinner and, once they'd finished eating, she and Spencer left for the Saunders' house. Paige could feel the panic creeping in. She finally found her opportunity when Levi excused himself to the restroom just as Bryce came back inside.

"They were running low on drinks," he explained, rummaging around the liquor cabinet. "We don't have much, but it's the neighborly thing to do."

"Do you mind stepping outside?" she asked. "There's something we need to talk about."

"I thought you'd never ask," Bryce said, following her over to the back patio without any of the bottles and shutting the door behind them. "By the way, Chris said everyone could come over if they wanted to…just not Levi."

"Bryce, this has to stop," Paige said. "You have to stop being so rude to Levi. You're making him feel unwelcome."

"I don't know what the problem is," he said, though she was sure he knew exactly what the problem was. "He wasn't invited here."

"Spencer invited him this morning to keep me company," Paige argued. "Bryce, this can't happen." She gestured in the space between them. "We've already cleared this up. The deal was that we could call this off at any time for any reason. If we keep trying to hang on, we'll ruin our friendship."

"You and I both know it was ruined a long time ago," Bryce said. "Do you want to know why I proposed the hookups in the first place? It was to show you how well we could work together. You're already my best friend, and I wanted more."

"Then why didn't you ask me to dinner like a normal person?"

"Because you wouldn't have agreed or taken me seriously. And, if I'm telling the truth here, I didn't think you'd agree to sleep with me. It was a suggestion to get you thinking about the possibility and see if there was any interest." His jaw clenched, and he took hold of her shoulders. "Paige, don't do this. Don't settle for someone you don't want because you think I'm going to hurt you. Have a little faith in me, please."

"This is my decision to make," she said. Already, her resolve was crumbling. "I like Levi—"

"And that's all," Bryce finished for her. "You like Levi, but there's no passion there. I know you've felt the same thing as me. There are questions and a lot of things to figure out, but I'm willing to do whatever it takes to be with you."

"Stop it," she hissed, but there was no power behind it. "I'm not doing this right now." *Although every bone in my body wants to kiss you.* "How would it look if we started dating? People will talk. They'll make up stories about what we mean to each other. Levi is like me. No one will ask questions."

"Why do you care?" Bryce asked, pulling her closer. Paige didn't pull away, following his touch. "It doesn't matter what anyone else thinks."

"I'm trying to protect you," she said, raising her voice. "It could ruin your reputation more. It could come back on your family and everything they've built. People still like to bring up what happened between Spencer and Stacy, and it always affects business. I couldn't do that to you."

"What if it means denying yourself what you really want?"

Paige couldn't answer that—it would ruin everything. She'd been trying to tuck her feelings away and build a wall around them, but it was starting to crumble. His very touch held more power than any kiss from Levi had. She reached for the doorknob, needing to get away before she could cave. Bryce pulled her back, bringing her face to his.

"Then say it," Bryce growled out. "Say that you want Levi and that you don't want me. Say it, and I'll never touch you again, I swear." His eyes softened and his voice lowered to a hoarse whisper. "I want this, Paige. I want you. I love to see you come alive. It's like watching someone strike a match in slow motion and letting it burn."

"Bryce," Paige said quietly. She couldn't pull away, didn't want to. She could have stayed there forever.

"No one else sees it, not Jade or Levi or you," he told her. "Now, tell me that you'd rather have Levi standing where I am, and I'll let go."

Bryce hovered out of reach and his message was clear. Paige would have to make the next move. She knew that the smart thing would be to say Levi's name, to get it over with and end the complicated triangle she'd wound up in. But Paige had never been known for doing the smart thing.

She rose up, meeting Bryce's soft lips and sighing as she wrapped her arms around his neck. This was what she wanted, and she was finally ready to admit it to herself. It felt almost *too* good to be pressed against Bryce's warmth, to have him hold her like there was no one else in the world.

It didn't matter what the future held. Hell, it didn't matter what the next ten minutes held. And maybe that was the secret. She didn't have to worry about what happened next, just about how life unfolded in the moment. Paige had known that at one point in her life, and that's what she'd lost. She'd worried so much about growing up that she'd lost sight of how to enjoy life as it was happening.

She backed away in time to see a shadow flicker over the door. "Levi," she said, releasing Bryce and rushing back into the house. Levi had already grabbed his coat and was headed toward the front entrance.

"Levi, I'm—"

"Sorry?" he finished for her. "Don't be. If he's the one you want, then more power to you. I wish you'd told me instead of stringing me along."

"Levi, please let me explain," she begged. "I didn't mean for this to happen. I wanted to tell you everything, and I will. Please, don't leave like this."

"I knew there was something between you two," he said, leaning on the occasional table near the front door. "I tried to tell myself that it was all him. And you... Why would you lead me on like this?"

She didn't have a good answer for him. She couldn't very well tell him that she was trying to settle for him, could she? It would sound worse to say that she was using him to get over Bryce.

"Be careful, Paige," Levi said. "I've lived around boys like that my whole life. Rich boys like to hide behind Daddy's money, spoiled to the point that they think they can get away with whatever they want. He's going to hurt you. You don't mean anything to him, but you do to me." He opened the door. "I'm not going to stand here and watch you go down this path. And I won't be there to pick up the pieces after."

"Please don't go back to New York," Paige said. "I know I have no right to ask it of you, but I want to make things right. I'm so sorry."

"I'm going to stay in town," he said, but he wouldn't meet her eye. "I need some time to think. And you clearly need time to prioritize." He didn't say goodbye, just slammed the door shut, making Paige jump.

She couldn't fool herself anymore. She didn't love Levi, not romantically, and the shame of what she had done gnawed at her. But he was her friend and she wanted to preserve that if she could. How had it all gotten so mixed up in five minutes? It only took one kiss from Bryce—

"Bryce." Paige looked over her shoulder to the open door and the empty patio. She raced outside, hoping that Bryce would be waiting on the steps or by the barrel, but he was nowhere to be seen. A loud yell from behind caught her attention, and she saw that their neighbors had started a fire of their own. Right there in the midst of it stood Bryce, his hands in his pockets as he casually chatted with one of the men.

He only went back to the party. Making things right started with being honest with Bryce. Tomorrow, she would be honest with Jade and Spencer and, once she'd figured out the right words, she would apologize to Levi. If he ended up not wanting her in his life anymore, then she would accept that.

She was making her way across the cool sand when she heard Bryce's name being called. From what she could see, a tall silhouette that could only be him was walking away from the firelight. He was walking toward her with a couple of people chasing after, combined with the flash of phones.

"Oh, no," she said, hurrying toward him. She could see Bryce's fists balled by his side, but he was too far away to make out his expression. Without warning, Bryce turned, swinging on the nearest person. He didn't make contact but knocked one of the phones to the ground. There was some yelling and arguing and, right as Paige got close, the man shoved Bryce.

Bryce staggered back but didn't fall. He laughed, bringing his fist to the man's jaw at lightning speed. The two exchanged blows, all the while cameras rolled on the spectacle.

"Stop it!" Paige found herself shouting.

It was the wrong thing to do. Bryce turned to her, his focus taken away as the stranger made contact with the side of his head. Bryce dropped to the ground before Paige could get to him. The crowd took the opportunity to run, holding up their phones as they went.

Bryce looked up at Paige blearily. He was resigned, as though he wanted the earth to swallow him up then and there. And Paige couldn't blame him. Those videos would go online, and he would be ruined. He was already on thin ice and, though she didn't know what had started the fight, she knew that viral videos rarely had much context.

"I'm sorry," he said in a strained voice. "I messed up, didn't I?"

"Don't worry about that right now," she said. "We'll know more tomorrow. Let's get you up, okay?"

She put an arm under his back and helped him into a sitting position. From there, she was able to get him to stand and walk with her, though he needed to lean heavily on her.

"He got me good," Bryce said. They were close enough to the house that she could already see a bruise starting to swell his right eye. His cheek was also reddened, and there was a cut on his left eyebrow, but it didn't look deep. She'd get to work with the first-aid kit when they got inside.

"That was reckless," she told him. "Why didn't you wait for me to come back?"

"I didn't know if you would." Bryce's voice sounded hollow. "I don't know what got into me."

"Do I need to take you to the hospital?"

"No," he said quickly. "Please, get me inside. I don't want Spencer to know yet."

The odds were good that those videos were being posted that very moment. And, if she knew Spencer half as well as she thought, he would have his phone set up to alert him when his brother hit the trending page. They made it up the steps and into the safety of the beach house. Paige locked the door and pulled all the shades down, including the ones that covered the back door. She grabbed the first-aid kit from the kitchen and started for Bryce's room. It was going to be a long night.

Chapter Fifteen

July 24

Paige set her phone down on the dresser. She couldn't look at it anymore. It had been a few hours of dozing off and refreshing her social media whenever she snapped awake. The slow trickle of news stories that had started popping up after they had gotten back to the house had avalanched. Now, Bryce and Paige were all over the internet. 'Bad Boy Bryce' was trending, with everyone claiming that he had started the fight unprovoked, but Paige didn't believe that for a second.

After Paige had patched Bryce up, she'd heard the lock turn on his door. All she could do was leave him to rest, but the guilt ate away at her. She hadn't been there when he'd needed her. She'd chased after Levi, and there was no telling what Bryce's state of mind would have been after that.

She avoided watching the videos. The pictures were bad enough. Paige had been pacing the room when she heard Jade and Spencer return. They had been giggling and whispering and, judging from the lack of panic and yelling, Paige could assume that they didn't know yet. Either that or Spencer was too angry to confront his brother and distracting himself with Jade.

The clock on Paige's nightstand told her that it was after midnight. She washed her face in the bathroom, rubbing futilely at the shadows already appearing under her eyes. Paige then tucked her robe around her pajamas and pulled her hair up in a loose bun.

The first-aid kit sat on her dresser, and she picked it up, leaving her phone right where it was. She'd check on Bryce before Spencer got to him, just to make sure that he was okay. There might not be a way to come back from what had happened. For the first time since coming to Miami, Bryce had made the news and in the worst way possible. It had been his last chance to prove himself.

Paige held the red plastic box to her chest and stepped into the hallway, knocking on Bryce's door.

"Come in," Bryce said from the other side. Paige turned the knob, letting out a breath when it was unlocked, and there he was, sitting on his bed wearing the same rumpled shirt and sand-dusted jeans. Paige was sure he was as tired as she felt.

Bryce's room was similar to hers, with darker walls and bedding and more pictures than paintings. As many times as she'd been in there, she'd never looked around. Scuba gear was piled in a chest in one corner, while a collection of stuffed animals sat on a shelf. Books were stacked against the wall and one lay open on top. The bedroom was more lived in, more Bryce's, and there was something about it that she liked.

"How did you know it was me?" Paige asked, setting the box on the bed.

"If it had been my brother, he wouldn't have bothered knocking." Bryce was glaring down at his phone, his expression bleak. The bruise around his eye was bad, but it hadn't swollen shut. And the cut on his brow, likely from the man's ring, was open again.

"I see you're here to play nurse," he said. His tone wasn't insulting. It was mostly exhausted.

"I wouldn't have to if you had behaved." Paige sat down next to him. She took his face in her hands, noting how his five o'clock shadow scraped her palm. "You'll live, as long as you stop picking fights."

She got to work, sorting out the supplies she'd need. Luckily, accidents happened all the time in the art world, and she was well practiced. She cringed, remembering the incident with a pallet knife that had sent her to the hospital. There was a white scar under her index finger that most people never noticed.

"It wasn't your best moment," she continued. "I don't understand why you do this. Why did you punch him? I can imagine how annoying it must have been to have a camera in your face, but you've never acted violently toward anyone. And when Spencer finds out..." She let the sentence hang between them. They both knew that it wouldn't be pretty.

"What do you want from me?" Bryce asked, emotion choking any malice from his voice.

"Better," Paige suggested, wiping at the dried blood in his hair. "I know you're better than this, Bryce. And maybe you should not go to any parties for a while?"

"That's no fun." Bryce winced as she dabbed the alcohol pad against the cut. "Miami has the best clubs in the world, and I haven't been to one this whole time."

"The bars and the girl chasing in New York, I can understand. But the fighting? That's new." She prepared a bandage. "You swung on someone earlier this year, but never made contact and Spencer pulled you away before anything could come of it. What were you trying to prove, anyway?" When he didn't answer, she decided to do something drastic. "Bryce, if you don't tell me everything, I swear I'll leave today and never speak to you again. I can't sit around and watch you destroy yourself."

"I wasn't trying to prove anything." Bryce pushed her hand away. "I've been preparing for this my whole life, to be ready for all this responsibility, but..." He fell back onto the bed, releasing a breath to the ceiling. "The pressure's getting to me. And seeing you run after Levi was it for me.

"When I was in school, I was so driven, so eager to learn. And I let it all get into my head. Everyone convinced me that I needed to have fun while I still could, so I started going to more parties. And, as you've seen, it's snowballed." His eyes closed and Paige braced herself for what might come next. "I don't want the job in Italy."

"What?" Paige hadn't been expecting him to say anything like that.

"I've always been compared to Spencer and my father. Most of the time it was a joke or someone didn't mean it, but that's how it's been. And it wasn't any different in college. I started to wonder if I'd ever really wanted anything or if I was just trying to get out of the

Alexander shadow. I kept screwing up without meaning to until I didn't have any control." He sat back up, finally able to look at Paige. "I don't think I know who I am anymore."

"I know how you feel," Paige said without thinking.

"I know." He reached over and took her hand. "I thought I knew what I wanted for so long. I don't want to turn into Spencer or Carlton. I want to leave behind my own legacy one day, but right now, I want you." He laughed. "It's all I could think about since I found out you were coming with us."

Paige gave him a sad smile and squeezed his hand. He was like her, trying to be his own person. She and Bryce were in the same boat, both with their lives yawning before them and the choices feeling like the wrong thing.

"You remember last Christmas, don't you?" he asked, a hint of sparkle back in his eyes.

"Yes, I remember," Paige said. "We briefly discussed it during your offer."

"Discussed isn't how I would put it. It was great, though. Canceled flights and Chinese food. Also, lying, cheating exes, but it was a fun time." He lifted his head. "You were there to help me get over Lisa. And I think when you kissed me, that was when I truly fell in love with you."

"Fell in…" Paige couldn't finish her thought. The air had left her lungs, and she couldn't seem to remember how to pull it back in. "You mean that as, like, a turn of phrase, right?"

"I wish I did," he told her. "It would be easier. I didn't know how to tell you, and I didn't think you would ever go for a guy like me. I'm a mess, Paige, as you've seen for yourself. I'm lost and stupid and you deserve someone who has it all together. But I'm also selfish and I want you, so there's that." He shrugged. "I guess we'll need to figure out —"

Before he could finish his thought, Paige had thrown the kit from her lap and fallen into him. He loved her. Bryce Alexander actually loved her — and Paige loved him. She pressed her lips against his in a desperate kiss, clutching his back and pulling him closer. It felt like she'd been in a freefall and suddenly her parachute had deployed. As Bryce kissed her back, holding her just as tightly, she felt secure and like she was exactly where she needed to be.

Bryce pulled back, his hand on her cheek. "I was so pissed at Levi," he said. "You went running after him, and I knew he'd say something to change your mind or make you rethink our kiss. I went back to the party, but there were these guys there who recognized me and started harassing me. Chris tried to get them to back off, but they wouldn't listen.

"They were pulling out their phones and I tried to get out of there, but they followed me." He paused. "I think I let Levi get into my head and took it out on the first person I saw. I swear, Paige. That's not me."

"I know it isn't," she said, smoothing his hair back. "I know." Bryce had a temper and was capable of throwing a tantrum better than most toddlers, but it never came to actual blows. Not unless someone else started it, and Paige had seen the other man make the first move.

"So," Bryce started slowly, "how is Levi?"

"He's…not happy. But, he said he'd stick around, so I might be able to fix this." Paige let her head fall to Bryce's shoulder. "I never felt romantically inclined to Levi. I think I was trying to get away from you and how you made me feel. I'm not sad about it, but I am worried that I'll lose a friend forever."

"Paige, I know that this is my fault." He gently pulled her up to face him. "And I wish I could take it all back and have a do-over. I should have said something to you sooner." He moved closer, removing the small space between them. "You are so amazing and beautiful, and I know that we could be perfect for each other if we tried. Actually tried, not just playing pretend."

"I… Bryce, I need to think about it," Paige said. "I love you, and it feels so good to admit it finally. But we have some things to figure out. We both need to decide on careers and where we would live. We'd also have to figure out how to tell Jade and Spencer. And, don't forget, you have to talk to Spencer about last night."

Bryce made a disgusted face. "I hear you, but can I ask one favor?"

"Anything," Paige said, and she meant it.

"Can we pretend one more time?" he asked. "I want one more night of you and me, without Levi or Spencer breathing down our necks or the internet blowing up with my fight video. I want to pretend like there isn't another soul on Earth and we have the rest of our lives to spend with each other. Would that be okay?"

Paige looked at him. There was something behind those eyes that hadn't been there in some time. After a few seconds had passed, she realized that she'd been staring without giving him an answer. Paige didn't speak. She sealed her lips over his, willing herself to comply and forget about who they were or what was happening out in the world. It was so much easier than it should have been.

Bryce reached up with both hands to cup her face and pull her closer. Paige sighed into the kiss, opening her mouth to accept more of him. There were no thoughts of right or wrong, of age gaps or childish crushes. It was her and Bryce, and it was the only thing in her life that made any sense. After weeks of feeling lost, she allowed herself to be found.

Paige delved a hand into Bryce's messy hair and pulled him down, lying back to that his comforting weight was on top of her. She didn't know what would happen when the sun came up. A meteor could strike and destroy the world before that happened. The most important thing was what she wanted in that moment, and it so happened to be the man pulling open her robe and sliding his warm hands over her skin.

The sheets tangled around them as, one by one, their clothes made their way to the floor. The morning would bring more problems for them both, but those problems could be figured out and they wouldn't last forever. Life would move on, and Paige was willing to let Bryce be her anchor, if only for that night.

Chapter Sixteen

Loud banging at the door startled Paige and Bryce awake. Paige's head swam as Bryce started to pull on his clothes, promising to be out in a second. She scooped her own clothes from the floor and had made it into the bathroom when Spencer wrenched the door open and charged into the room. Paige slid behind the door where she was able to see most of the room through the crack.

"I don't want to hear you try to explain yourself," Spencer growled, his back to her. Paige would have felt better if he had shouted. "Dad is flying in today and he said that we have to be home before dark."

"What?" Bryce asked, jumping over the bed. She could see that his eye was bruised a shiny purple, but he looked better than he had the night before.

"Don't act surprised," Spencer said. "You've blown your last chance. I'm not backing you up this time."

"I don't need you to back me up," Bryce sneered. "I'll talk to Dad and get this sorted out on my own. You stay here with Jade."

"I have to go with you," Spencer said, his tone softening ever-so slightly. "He's taking away your position at the company. I'll be there for business, not as your brother."

Bryce blinked. He didn't seem to be worried or upset. He'd admitted to her that he didn't want the job, but it must have been a shock for Carlton to actually take it away. "What's next?"

"Pack your things," Spencer said. "We'll be leaving as soon as you're ready. And you might want to apologize to Paige before we go."

"Paige?"

"She saved your ass last night, but that put her in the spotlight. There are already rumors about you two going around, and I don't think she'll appreciate that. So, yes, apologize for dragging her into your mess and sort this out with the press later, okay? She doesn't deserve it."

Spencer turned away from Bryce, and Paige heard the door shut after him. Bryce sat down on the bed, staring at where his brother had stood. She wanted to say something, but what could she say? All she could do was look into Bryce's shattered blue eyes from her hiding place behind the door. She expected to see tears, but there was only emptiness. She finally stepped out from around the door but stayed on the cool tile.

"Bryce," she said, so quiet that she wasn't sure if she'd spoken out loud. "Bryce, what can I do to help?"

"I guess I need to pack," he said. He stood up and took his suitcase from the closet. "Why did you hide, anyway?"

"I figured Spencer would be angry enough as it was. I didn't want him getting any more upset. I think we should tell him in our own time." She took a few steps closer, her clothes held tight to her chest. "Are you sure there's nothing I can do for you?"

"No," he said sharply. "I don't want you getting any more involved than you already are." His eyes were soft as he tried his best to smile. "I'm sorry, Paige...for all of it. Please, let me sort this out, okay?"

"You don't need to apologize, but I trust you." She wrapped her robe around herself, crossing the room to kiss Bryce's cheek before leaving the room. It was a hard thing to do, but she understood that he needed space.

As Paige would soon discover, once she was dressed and pretending to leave her room that morning, Jade was in no state to fly and would be staying in Miami. Spencer made arrangements for her to follow the next day, and Paige was told to stay in the beach house as long as she wanted. Once that was settled, Spencer led the way out to the car while Bryce stopped, suitcase in hand, and gave Paige one last smile before closing the door behind him.

Paige was grateful that Jade was still there. She didn't want to be alone in the house and it didn't feel so empty with Jade upstairs. There was too much to think about, and the last thing that Paige needed was space to think. She'd just settled onto the couch, TV remote in hand, when there was a knock on the door.

Paige flew from the couch, hoping that it would be Bryce there to kiss her senseless once again and assure her that nothing had changed between them. He'd only given her a casual goodbye under Spencer's watch before leaving. But she had asked that they keep their relationship private until they could figure it out, a decision that she was already regretting.

Paige swung open the door, heat washing over her into the cool house, and was shocked to see Levi before her. Her face fell, and she felt her smile dissolve.

"I passed Spencer's car on the way in, and he did *not* look happy," Levi said. "I was worried that you were leaving, too, after what happened."

"You heard?" she asked, the shame of the night before clouding her words. "I wouldn't have left without telling you." They stood there, Paige hanging out of the open door and Levi shuffling his feet awkwardly. She took a deep breath and noticed that Levi was wearing that damned Kilian cologne that reminded her of Bryce.

"I wanted to see if you were ready to talk." Levi winced at his own words. "There's a lot to say and I know you like to procrastinate. I'd like it if you'd let me inside, though."

"Of course, come in." She opened the door wider, allowing him in. She didn't know what to say to him other than the truth. But, after everything she'd put him through, it was what he deserved.

"How much longer will you be in town?" Levi asked as he followed her to the sunroom.

"I'm not sure," she told him. "Jade's flying back in the morning, but they told me I could stay as long as I like." She sat on the hammock, gently rocking back and forth, while Levi occupied an armchair near the window. "I assume you'll be leaving soon?"

"There's nothing to keep me here anymore," Levi said with sincerity. "And I wanted to apologize for everything."

"You don't have anything to apologize for," Paige said. "I'm the one who's sorry. I led you on, and that was so wrong of me. I don't expect you'll want to be my friend after this."

"We'll always be friends, Paige. I'm hurt and I'll be distant, but let me get over you and things can go back to normal, I promise." He leaned forward, his elbows on his knees. "I'm sorry for pressuring you. I knew there was something between you and Bryce, but I'm so used to getting what I want that I thought I could change your mind. Showing up here like I did wasn't right."

"I guess we both acted like jerks, huh?" She was only half joking. "What are you going to do now?"

"I guess I'll go home," Levi said, focusing on one of the plants in the corner. "The city here is nice, but it isn't New York. It doesn't inspire the same way."

"What do you mean?" Paige asked, bringing her knees up to her chest.

"I'm not saying that it's a dump," Levi said with a small laugh. "I'm saying that it's not my scene. There's something about the sun coming up over the bay in New York, the way the light sparkles over the buildings."

"You do know that the same thing happens here, right?"

"It seems...warmer. I know that sounds weird, but it's not the same."

"It makes perfect sense." Paige smiled at him. "It's part of the reason I love this place so much. I did my worst work in New York. This place, the culture and life, makes Miami special. I should have come back a long time ago."

"Despite everything, I'm glad you came to New York instead." Levi was quiet. "I need to hear you say that you don't want the job, that you don't want me."

Paige's face gave her away before her words could. It hurt more than she could describe. She knew that Levi was a treasure and any woman would be lucky to have him, but it wouldn't be her.

"Paige," Levi whispered, "it's okay." His forced smile said otherwise, but she let him continue. "I want you to be happy. And I want you to stop making other people's feelings a priority over yours. I don't care if it means I go home alone. I want you to be happy."

"I'm sorry," she said. "Not for my decision, but for hurting you. You're my friend, Levi, and I want you to be happy, too. But you wouldn't be happy with me. There's someone else out there who will love you the way you deserve."

Levi's smile lost some of its sadness, and he stood. "I'll be sure and keep an eye out." He leaned over to kiss Paige's forehead. "Could you do something for me? If I'm going out to look for someone new, I want you to do the same."

"Levi, I know you don't like Bryce, but he's a great guy." She felt her heart warm ever-so-slightly. "He loves me."

"I've done my own research." Levi looked down at her with concern. "I don't know that I trust him."

"I've seen the trending page and it always twists things around. I was there last night, and it didn't go down the way they're saying."

"I believe you." Levi raised his hands in surrender. "I have a flight to catch, but I hope I can see you soon?"

"Of course. I might have a new piece for your gallery the next time you see me."

"There will always be a spot for you on my wall." Levi wrapped her up in a hug and Paige felt like everything was going to be alright.

Levi started for the door but stopped before stepping out. "It won't be easy."

"What?"

"The two of you. People will talk. They already are. You'll be blamed for his actions and anything you accomplish will be attributed to him, good or bad. It's going to make life harder for the both of you."

Paige thought about it. Did the risks outweigh the rewards? "I think I'm up to the challenge."

Levi grinned. "Whatever works for you. See ya."

Once Levi was gone and the red Wrangler had pulled away, Paige settled back onto the couch with her phone. She hadn't bothered checking it that morning, but she was curious. Bryce was still trending, but so was she. Paige sat up straighter, scrolling through pictures of herself, Jade and Clint. People were already drawing the lines between Paige and the Alexanders, and they didn't seem too happy about it. The top of the page was dominated by a picture of her on the beach, staring straight into the camera with a horrified expression as Bryce lay in the sand.

Spencer and Bryce's earlier comments made sense. Already, the public was calling her a cougar, a gold-digger, someone using Bryce for her own gain. And they were calling Bryce an idiot for falling for it. Paige tried to swallow, but her mouth was dry.

Paige quickly pulled up an app on her phone and called for a ride. Spencer had called a car earlier to take him to the airport, which meant that there was a vehicle at the house. But, since she was going alone, she wanted to make sure Jade had a way to get away if she needed to.

Once the ride was pulling onto her street, Paige threw her phone in her purse and slung it over her shoulder. "I'm going out for a bit," she yelled up the stairs, hoping that Jade could hear her. She'd spent too much time in that house already. She had to get away.

The ferry to the mainland was more crowded than it had been in a while, and Paige tried her best to make herself small. It was hard to do in a bright, rainbow-patterned maxi-dress, but she was doing her best. She settled into her seat and a small *ping* made her take her phone back out. Bryce was going live.

Paige stared, her lips pressed tightly together, as she watched Bryce adjust himself in front of the camera. She recognized the headrest of the jet behind him. They were on their way to New York. Spencer was nowhere to be seen, but Bryce looked like he was about to throw up, and she could imagine that his brother sat on the other side of the phone. She'd never seen Bryce in such a state.

Thousands of viewers were already tuned in to watch, and comments were popping up so quickly that she couldn't read them, not that she wanted to. The only words she cared about were Bryce's. Had he seen the articles and posts yet?

"Hey, guys," he started awkwardly. "I know you've all seen what happened, and I know I've let a lot of people down. I wanted so badly to prove that I was better than the media portrayed me, and I failed. But that's not what this is about." He paused and she could see a flash of pain in his eyes. "You can come after me for being irresponsible and a bad influence all you want, but please stop involving my family and other innocent people who are trying to help me through this."

Paige felt her heart seize. This was about her. It had probably been Spencer's idea.

"Paige Montgomery has nothing to do with me," Bryce said. "She's my sister-in-law's best friend who was trying to watch out for me. I know it can be fun to sensationalize everything for views and clicks, but this needs to stop. There is nothing between Paige and me, and there never will be."

"Bryce," Paige said, staring down at her phone as tears pooled in her eyes. She knew that he had to say it, that Spencer was watching and wouldn't allow another slip-up to get in their way. But he said it with such conviction that it seemed like the truth.

"I'm only going to say this once, because she doesn't deserve this," Bryce said. "Paige Montgomery means nothing to me."

Chapter Seventeen

The cab pulled up to the curb, and Paige stepped out onto the sidewalk. Dozens of bodies pushed their way past her, all crowding to the shops and restaurants on the strip. Little Havana was different from the time Bryce had brought her there. Everyone was in a rush, either on their lunch break or heading back to work. Only a couple of bands played in the streets, but the power was still in the air.

Paige thought she knew what loss felt like. She'd been feeling it for over a year, the loss of her passion and drive, and she thought that was the worst it could get. She'd started to find herself, her true self, and she'd done that with Bryce at her side. And, yes, she was feeling betrayed, but she knew why he'd said what he had about her. He was trying to protect her from the media.

It wasn't easy being romantically attached to an Alexander. Jade had only mentioned it once to Paige, but being married to Spencer made it difficult to form friendships with others in her field. Granted, Spencer was considered a celebrity — there were fans and letters and that was all for the one who stayed out of the tabloids. Being linked publicly to Bryce would have Paige front and center for some time.

But the memories of the night before clung to her skin. She loved Bryce, and he loved her. He'd said so himself. And he'd shown her into the early hours of the morning how much he'd meant it. When she thought about it, any price seemed worth paying to have that again, even if it was just one more time.

"Maybe it's for the best," she said out loud. Saying it gave it more power, and she hoped she'd be able to convince herself. She'd allowed herself to believe, while Bryce held her close and kissed her, that they could have it all without any repercussions. But Levi had been right. They might manage to work it out, but it would never be easy. They were both lost and broken, and they would destroy each other if they tried to force a real relationship too early.

Paige stood before Slice of Lime, which was unusually empty. Most of the patrons, she assumed, had already enjoyed their meals and left. Bussers were taking up dishes and wiping down tables while some employees took their own breaks at the bar. There were no twinkly lights or live bands, but there were a handful of people and the hum of everyday life around her.

"*Buenos tardes!*" She recognized the waiter from the other night, waving to her from behind the register, and he apparently remembered her. "Grab any seat you like," he told her. "I'll be with you in a moment."

It hadn't been her intention to go there. She didn't know why she'd given the name of the place to the cabbie. But she took a seat at the same corner table where she'd sat with Bryce and picked up a menu. She stared at it without reading when a small scream caught her attention. She turned to see a couple of kids running past with water guns.

Behind them, the boy who'd encouraged her to paint with him was busy spraying streaks over one of the walls. She watched him move with ease, the way he was able to blend the colors and the shapes together to form something truly beautiful, and she was envious. She was angry. And, more than anything else, she wanted to paint.

"Will your gentleman friend be joining you today?" The waiter's question pulled her back to where she was, and she turned sharply.

"Excuse me?" she asked before realizing he was asking about Bryce. "Oh, no, he won't. It's just me today."

"No, it's not." This time, Paige was surprised by a new voice. Jade set her purse on the ground and took the seat across from her. "I'll have a glass of water, please. Give us a minute to look over the menu?"

"Sure thing." The waiter nodded before slipping back behind the counter.

"What are you doing here?" Paige asked, though it was obvious. "Did you follow me? That's touching, if not unsettling, Jade."

"I followed you to the ferry," Jade told her. "I knew it was creepy and I was going to turn around, but I'd already come so far. I wasn't ready for this, though." She thanked the waiter who handed her a glass of ice water and took a long drink. "I heard what you and Levi talked about."

"Oh, you're eavesdropping, too? This feels stalker-y." She laughed lightly.

"Well, the two of you weren't exactly whispering." She gave Paige a small smile. "When were you going to tell me about Bryce?"

"I wanted to," Paige said, "but I didn't know how. I wasn't sure of my own feelings until last night. It's been a confusing few weeks, Jade, and I should have come to you about all of it sooner. I think I was scared of what you would think."

"I wish you had," Jade said. "We might have been able to avoid a lot of this." She leaned back in her chair. "Will you tell me everything now? I want to know what exactly happened with you and Bryce. And if you could include how Levi fit into it all, that would be nice."

The words might have stung if Jade hadn't offered a good-natured laugh. She could understand Jade not being able to put all the pieces together — all this was so unlike the Paige that she knew. She stole a sip of Jade's water before beginning with her story.

Paige told Jade everything, all about her doubts and Bryce's offer. She shared how Bryce had ended up helping her find herself and opened up about his own troubles. She told her about the time they'd spent together and about how she'd fallen harder for Bryce than she'd thought was humanly possible.

She ended her tale with the video that she'd watched on the ride over. To her credit, Jade didn't interrupt once, and she kept a calm composure. She let Paige talk until she ran out of words then thought for a while.

"Paige, I'm going to start by saying that I don't care if you sleep with Bryce, but I don't think you two should date yet. From what I've seen, you've been good for him, but neither of you are where you need to be for this kind of relationship right now. Bryce's path will see him cut off from his family before he's thirty if he keeps it up. Yours will have you seeking purpose until the search crushes you, and you give up on everything."

"Don't sugarcoat it for me." Paige sighed and let her head fall into her hands. "I know that we could crash and burn. I told Bryce the same thing. I know we have a lot to fix before we can be who the other needs us to be, but when I'm with him, I feel like myself. I can't explain it, but it's like he brings out the real me. He lets me express myself in a way that no one else does."

"Well, that hurts."

"Oh, no, Jade, that's not what I meant."

"I know, hon. I've shared things with Spencer that I haven't with another living person," Jade said with a shrug. "That's what happens when you find someone you love."

"When I was with Levi, I felt like I was putting on a mask. It was like pretending to be someone I'm not, the person that everyone expects. And when I'm not pretending, I don't know who I am. But, with Bryce…" She let the sentence hang in the air.

"I'm not going to tell you that I predicted this." Jade leaned forward with her elbows on the table. "I'm honestly impressed that you two managed to keep this a secret. I mean, the way you acted around each other gave me some idea, but I didn't know it had gone so far." She laughed. "I remember the way y'all flirted when you first met, and I thought that was just how it was between you."

"It was at first," Paige said. "I was infatuated, but this is something new. It turned into a real thing. I'd never imagined how this would turn out, either."

"I support you both, as long as it's what you want." She reached over and took Paige's hand. "I'm your friend, and I want you to be happy, no matter what, okay? We've been together since middle school, and nothing will change that. I think it would be smart for you to wait, but I do want what's best for you."

Paige squeezed her hand in response. Her throat closed as a sob worked its way up through her lips, but she forced the words out. "Jade, I don't know what will make me happy. I don't know what I want or what I'm supposed to do now. I've been floundering here, and Bryce and this place have changed everything, but I don't know who I am." She looked over at the street artist who continued to work, creating his masterpiece.

"I know who you are." Jade's tone got Paige's attention. "You're Paige Montgomery. You're my best friend, a loyal and beautiful person who I am proud to know. You're inspiring and talented and one of the few people left in this world who believes magic exists and is able to prove it with a brush and some paint. I love you, Paige…and so does Bryce.

"He'll need you." Jade closed her eyes. "Whether it's as a friend or something else, Bryce is going to need you soon. And you need him, too." She turned back to Paige. "You might both be lost and trying to figure yourselves out, but you have a way of helping each other through that. All he needs is a little time."

"I would like to think we have a future together," Paige said. "It's the biggest risk I've ever taken, and it's scary and unreliable, but I trust it. And I do think it's in the cards for us one day."

"If you trust it, I trust it." Jade stood with her bag looped over her arm. "I'll let you figure out the rest. I'll be at the house when you need me."

"You're not staying?" Paige thought about standing and leaving with her. She didn't want to be alone.

"I think you need some time to yourself. You have a lot to think about, and I don't want to influence anything."

"It's a bit late for that, don't you think?"

"Okay, here's some more for you. What Spencer says goes. You don't have to come back to New York with me tomorrow. You know what? I don't want you to. I want you to stay right here and paint me something, okay? You know where that cute craft store is, and you have my express permission to raid their paint section."

"Thank you," Paige said, feeling another welling of tears.

Jade leaned down and kissed her forehead, in almost the exact same spot as Levi had. She didn't say anything else and left Paige sitting at the table alone. But Paige didn't feel lonely. She felt like she could see a direction, a path forming in front of her, new and exciting and leading somewhere unknown.

Paige looked over at the young man. He was adding the finishing touches to his mural. It was a cityscape that included a dancing couple with fireworks exploding in the sky above them. She smiled. Maybe she was getting swept up in the moment, but the couple reminded her of herself and Bryce.

Paige finally ordered her meal and reached into her bag to pull out her sketchbook and pencils. She tossed her phone in its place, zipping the purse shut. Her fingers ached with the need to draw and create something. And it wasn't another abstract piece that she had in mind.

In her head, Paige could picture the perfect scene, the perfect piece, that would put her on the map for the right reasons. She could forget about Bryce for a bit. She could forget about how she'd broken Levi's heart. And the weight of keeping secrets from her best friend was lifted, so what did she have to worry about? She began to sketch.

There was plenty left for her to figure out, and she would need to call Bryce soon to check on him. Or she would wait for him to call first. If time was what he needed, then that was what she'd give him. For now, there was only the idea swirling around her like the scents of Little Havana, begging her to bring something new to life.

Chapter Eighteen

August 12

Paige's canvas spanned the entire wall. It was ten feet tall and almost thirteen feet wide, the biggest piece she'd ever created. It had been specially delivered to the Alexanders' beach house, and Paige had been able to work on it whenever she liked. There had been plenty of plastic spread over the living room floor to protect the wood, and the light coming through the giant windows was exactly what she needed.

"I had to keep the doors open so the house was ventilated," Paige said, longing to reach out and touch the textured canvas. There were silver chains keeping everyone away from the art, including the artists themselves. "I had to wear a mask the whole time I was using spray paint, but being able to hear the ocean helped."

"I can imagine." Levi wrapped an arm around her shoulders. "What made you think of it?"

She smiled at him. Levi had actually dressed for the occasion, sporting a burgundy dinner jacket and black button-down that was open at the throat. His black pants were distressed and torn, but his long braids were pulled back and he'd trimmed his beard close. Paige could appreciate the effort.

"Like I told you, Miami inspired me." Paige beamed with pride at her work. It was another abstract painting with a clearly defined silhouette of her own body that had been a pain to create. Inside was a foggy gray landscape with a dark road that vanished into the distance. Around her, vibrant colors brought the city she loved to life. She could pick out the cafe, with its rust browns and bright yellows, and the purples and oranges that made up the sunset. It was blocks of color that came together in a brilliant kaleidoscope.

"The skyline is a nice touch," Levi said. "I don't think it's lost on anyone. This is your most literal piece to date, not that it's a bad thing," he was quick to add. "It's not your standard thing, though."

"You're right," Paige told him. "But this is me, at least for now. And I take it as a compliment that my style is changing. I'm changing." She scrunched up her nose. "I think for the first time in my life."

"Are you sure this is the last piece you'll do for me?" Levi asked. "There's a lot of buzz around you, and it's not about Bryce anymore." He nodded to the crowd behind her. "Everyone wants your art in their home."

"We'll see," Paige said.

Levi squeezed her closer. It was nice to be back to old times with him. And she didn't need to worry about his feelings for her anymore. He'd started talking more and more about an art critic who'd made it her job to insult him. Paige could see something starting there, but she didn't want to ask about it and potentially ruin anything growing between them.

The point she focused on was that Levi was over her and she was over him—and that was what mattered. Paige stared at the painting before her. More than Miami, it made her think about Bryce. It was all there before her and, if she closed her eyes, she was right back there, dancing in the street with Bryce.

"Have you talked to him yet?" Levi asked.

"Who?" She cut her eyes over to him and back to the painting quickly. The topic of Bryce Alexander was a sore spot for her, especially coming from Levi. When she'd returned to New York, she'd reached out to Bryce, hoping that it would be her chance to work things out between them. He'd been polite yet distant and, following Jade's advice, Paige hadn't pushed him.

Now they were at the point where they would check up on each other every couple of days, but it was through short messages. She hadn't seen him since he'd left, but she thought about him every day. Patience had never been her strongest point, and she was doing well not to go to his apartment and knock the door down.

"I'm sure he'll come to his senses soon," Levi said, the remorse evident in his tone.

"One can only hope," Paige said in a low voice. "Have you talked to him since everything?"

"A couple of times," he told her, and it surprised her. "We'll have to wait and see what the future holds, I guess."

Paige couldn't have agreed more. She smoothed out the layered rainbow-colored skirts of her ball gown. Her black velvet bodice had matching rainbow sleeves that fell from her shoulders. She felt overdressed, but it was something she was comfortable in. It was her last gallery showing for a long time, after all, and she wanted to feel special. She'd made a vow to herself that she would no longer force herself to blend in with the crowd.

"So, what's next for you, Miss Montgomery?" Levi asked, breaking the silence.

Paige thought about it. Jade had told her that the Miami house was hers for as long as she needed if she wanted it. There was also her apartment in Texas that was waiting for her. Maybe she could convince her parents to let her use their garage to paint like she'd done in high school.

"I don't know," she said slowly and, as she spoke, a smile spread over her face. "I have options, but I don't need to make a decision now, so I'm not going to."

That was okay. And, for once, it wasn't something that she was telling herself. It was okay that she would change in the future. She'd finally figured out who she was. Paige Montgomery was a human—incomplete, ever-evolving and unsure. And it was fine.

Levi had just released her when one of the attendants stepped forward to place a placard under her painting that read 'Sold'. Paige brightened but couldn't help feeling sad. She was glad that it had sold, and she would be leaving tonight with a check, but she had wanted to hold on to the work and keep it as a reminder of her time in Florida with Bryce.

"Congratulations," Levi leaned in to whisper. "I think Mr. Alexander is pleased with his purchase."

Paige looked over at Spencer and Jade, both dressed like royalty, and Jade with her baby bump extended. Spencer raised his champagne glass to her and she grinned.

"I thought after he found out about the paint fumes stinking up his house, he'd never want to see this thing again." She laughed and hugged Levi. "It doesn't match anything else in their penthouse," she said, almost as an afterthought. "I wonder where he'll hang it."

"I'll make room for it somehow," Bryce said. Paige released Levi and spun to face Bryce. He, too, was in a navy-blue tux that complemented his eyes and dark hair, holding a bouquet of wildflowers. "I'm not interrupting anything, am I?"

"I think you're right on time," Levi said, reaching out to shake Bryce's free hand. "I'm glad to see you got my invitation, even if you didn't get back to me until the last minute."

"I've been busy," Bryce said. Paige could sense that there was still tension between them, though she was sure it would fade with time. The fact that they had been in contact with each other at all was surprising to her.

Bryce had that goofy grin on his face as he held the flowers out to Paige. "I remember you mentioning that you couldn't decide on your favorite flower, so I brought a variety," he said.

"I remember mentioning that to *Jade* at one point," Paige retorted, taking the flowers and bringing them to her nose. "You bought the painting?"

"I had to," he told her, gesturing around them. "I didn't know how this was going to go, so I had to have something to remember you by in case...y'know, this didn't work." He nodded to Levi, who took the hint and left to speak to another artist.

"Would it be okay if we talked?" Bryce asked, offering her his arm.

Paige clutched the flowers close to her chest. She wanted to slap his arm away and wrap herself around him. She wanted to hold on tight and never let go. She wanted to tell Bryce that she loved him and missed him. But she held back and accepted his arm. *Has he ruined me this much?*

They began to walk away from the painting, making their way past other pieces and the attendees discussing them. Bryce started talking to her in a low voice, so as to not be overheard.

"I'm sorry I haven't been talking to you," he said. "I wanted to see you as soon as you got into town. I kept going by the penthouse, hoping you would be there. But, when I found out you were staying in Miami until the show, I thought you were trying to avoid me. I know what I said must have upset you, and I'm sorry for that, too."

"I needed some time to think," Paige said. "I'm sure you did, too."

Bryce nodded. "I think I've got what I needed figured out," he said. "At least, I hope I have. And, I really am sorry —"

"Please," she interrupted, stopping them mid-step, "don't try and explain. I do understand why you did what you did, and I'm not mad. I know you were protecting me, and it worked, for the most part. I was off the trending page before the end of the week."

"It doesn't make any of it fair, though," Bryce said. He began to walk again, taking her with him. "And I could have done more. You don't know how many times I started to book a ticket back to Miami."

"How did you know I was staying at the beach house?"

"I, uh, begged Jade to tell me," he said sheepishly. "I think she felt bad for me."

Paige held back a giggle. He *had* been thinking about her all that time. "At the risk of sounding pathetic, if you'd ever reached out and asked to see me, I would have flown back the second my phone rang."

"I'm sorry." Bryce winced. "That's all I can say."

"Bryce, what happened after you came back to New York?" Paige asked. "It didn't seem right to ask Jade or Spencer, and I wanted to hear it from you."

Bryce turned the corner, taking them down another hall with rows of sculptures. There weren't as many people on that side of the gallery, as they were all taking their time observing the other paintings. Paige was grateful for the solitude, and she was sure Bryce was, too.

"Spencer wouldn't talk to me for the entire plane ride," Bryce said. "He asked me to make things right with you, then it was all silence. The same when Dad got here. They both left me in the penthouse while they went to have their talk. After about an hour, they finally came to hear my side of things."

"And?"

"I told the truth," he said. "I hadn't realized how tired I'd been of the lying. I didn't want to move to Italy, and I didn't want to take over another branch of the company my brother owns." He had started to speak louder, his words becoming impassioned. "I finally admitted to both of them how sick I was of being the dutiful son, always being compared to Spencer and supposed to accept it with a smile. And I told them how I knew that I was acting childish, but I didn't know how else to express what I was feeling."

Bryce became quiet for a long while before continuing. "I was so scared that Dad would be ashamed of me or disappointed like he usually is — and he was. He started out by telling me how let down he felt by my actions and that the immaturity of it all did make him ashamed. I got the whole 'he raised me better than that' speech." The last bit was done in a scarily accurate impression of Carlton.

"But then he told me that he was proud of me," he said. "He was proud that I was finally standing up for myself and what I wanted. He did feel the need to let me know I didn't know what that was or how to express myself. But then, he hugged me." Bryce smiled. "I couldn't remember the last time my dad had hugged me, Paige."

He'd finally stopped calling his father Carlton, which had to have meant that some part of their relationship had been repaired. She smiled, leaning into him more. They turned another corner, wrapping back around to the paintings.

"All this is to say that I won't be moving to Italy," Bryce said. "I'm here to stay. The position has been offered to someone else, and I know she'll do a good job. It also gives me time to put my own plans into action and start making a name for myself."

"Where are you going to start?" Paige asked. She was glad that he'd figured out so much in such a small amount of time. They slowed to a stop, back in front of Paige's painting, which had drawn quite a crowd.

"I'm going to start right here, if I can," he said, pulling her closer to him. "I was an idiot who didn't know what he was doing before. I'm sorry for what I put you through. I hope you can forgive me?"

"I've already told you that there's nothing to forgive," she whispered. "We were both stupid and lost and trying to use each other in our own way."

"Do you think it's possible to give this another chance?" Bryce pressed his forehead to hers. "I know that people will talk, and I understand if you don't want to be involved. I want your honest answer."

"Only if you give me yours first," Paige countered. "I know that I love you, Bryce, and I will give you everything I have. Tell me why we should do this when we can stay friends and write the whole thing off." It cut her deep to bring it up, but she had to know that he was serious about her. Maybe it was her old insecurities coming up, but she had to hear it. "Why do you want this?"

"Are you kidding me? Paige, you're everything I want." Bryce smiled at her. "Ever since I met you, I knew you were something special. I'm okay with staying friends if you are, but I'll always want more. I can't imagine the rest of my life without you in it."

"And the sex isn't bad, either, right?" Paige laughed and closed the short distance between their lips, sealing her mouth over his. She'd already decided that she didn't care what it took, she would find her way back to Bryce. He was the only person who saw her, truly saw her, for who she was. He pushed her outside her comfort zone and made her a better person.

She knew that it wouldn't be easy. She would be recognized as the girl from the beach, and it was likely to start a whole new wave of rumors when they went public, but they could deal with it together.

"I love you, Bryce," she said. "I don't know exactly when it happened or how, but I'm in love with you, and

I don't care what happens tomorrow, as long as you're next to me."

"Well, with this sale, you're free to do whatever you want," Bryce said, facing the painting. "What will your next project be?"

"I don't know," she said with a shrug. "Isn't that fantastic?"

Bryce grinned, wrapping his arms around her waist and pulling their bodies flush. The onlookers were forgotten. The gallery, the painting, all of it faded away as Bryce kissed her again.

Chapter Nineteen

September 21

Paige didn't think she would ever get used to waking up next to Bryce. A month had passed, and there had been time before that, but it always felt like waking up on Christmas morning. Paige naturally got up earlier than he did, so she would usually lie there, rubbing small circles on his chest while he slept. Once the curtains began glowing with morning light, she would get up and step onto the patio to watch the sun come up over the ocean.

It had taken a lot of talking for them to convince each other that moving in together wasn't a mistake. The beach house was big enough that they could have space when they wanted, so it was an obvious choice. They were in their trial period, but there was so much uncertainty with everything else that one more experiment couldn't hurt.

Paige had reclaimed her guest room, moving the heavy furniture out with Bryce's help. The floors were covered with white sheets, already stained with paint, and the walls were lined with canvases. Many of the paintings were half-finished, but she liked it that way. If she got stuck on one, she would move on to another. Paige wasn't about to get linger in a rut again.

Bryce had been hard at work in the downstairs office, busy drawing up the paperwork for a new gallery. It had been something they'd come up with during their first week back in Miami. He was starting an investment firm, something that he called a 'stepping stone' to something larger that he hadn't quite pinpointed yet. And Paige had the perfect idea for his first major investment.

A community art center was being built on the mainland under Paige's name. It would be a place for anyone to come and express themselves and would have a gallery to feature local street artists. Bryce had handled the investors and most of the business side, while Paige had been working to garner interest from the cities.

"It's not what I had in mind when I said I wanted to make a name for myself," Bryce had said, staring up at the white brick building, "but it's a start."

Paige curled up on the lounge chair, listening to the soothing sound of the gulls and the waves. She could almost go back to sleep if she wanted. But that day was special. It was the first day that she and Bryce were taking off from work to spend together. She was worried that they'd been burying themselves in the art center to avoid each other and the strangeness that comes with a new relationship, and today would prove that one way or another.

Paige's phone pinged from the table next to her and she picked it up. Clint was starting a video chat with her and Jade. Paige brushed back her new pixie-cut hair, complete with pink streaks, and swiped the screen to answer. The screen was split with Clint and Jade smiling back at her.

Jade was positively glowing, as she had been since their vacation, and it was obvious from the dirt smeared on Clint's cheek that he'd already been hard at work.

"I didn't know if you'd be up, Paige," Clint said with his thick Texas drawl. "I'm glad you are."

"How could I miss this? It's been forever since we've talked. How are you feeling, Jade?"

"Bloated, tired, hungry and elated," she said, though she looked like none of those things. "You name it, and I feel it. How's Miami?"

"It's great, as usual." Paige pulled her knees up to her chest. "But we're forgetting Clint. He's the one who called this meeting. What's up?"

"Can't I want to see you guys?" Clint asked innocently. "Does there have to be an ulterior motive?"

"I'm not buying it," Jade said, lying back on the couch. "Tell us what's going on."

"You act like it's bad news, but it's actually great. You two are the first to know that Kindall and I have set a date for the wedding."

"So soon?" Paige asked.

"You know Kindall. She's already planning everything out. She's over at Karmen's vineyard making arrangements, and the wedding isn't until May."

"That sounds like her," Jade said.

"Clear your calendars for May 12. You'll both need to be in Texas, because I think y'all are going to be bridesmaids." Clint's name was called from somewhere behind him, and Paige figured out that he was hiding in a barn.

"Are you running away from your job?" she asked.

"They can handle things for a while. I want to know how my girls are doing."

They allowed Clint to play hooky as they caught up over the next hour. Paige told them about her latest paintings and the art center, Jade shared the strangest cravings she'd had and how much she missed work and Clint could only talk more about Kindall and the wedding.

They hadn't sat down and talked together in several months and Paige felt the pang of missing her friends. They were all living in different states and living different lives than they had been a few years ago. A warm feeling spread in her chest, overtaking the sadness. For those few minutes, laughing with her friends, it was like old times again.

Clint was eventually found and dragged out of the barn he'd snuck away to, and Jade had to go get brunch. Paige said her goodbyes, putting her phone down to stare back at the ocean. What would she be doing with her day off?

"Don't look so angry," Bryce's groggy voice said behind her. "You always look so angry when you think."

"I do not," Paige protested. "I look deep and pensive."

Bryce snorted and sat next to her. "I already feel like a failure for taking the day off," he said. "It's like I'm slipping into old habits, and I hate it."

"I get that," Paige said. "When you've spent so long being productive, it's weird to take a break. But, if anyone's earned it, it's you."

"You mean us," he corrected. "You've been working as hard as I have. Is there anything you want to do today?"

"We could go to King Unlimited, and I could obliterate you in laser tag—unless you're too scared."

"It's Thursday," he said. "They're open to the public, so it might be a little crowded. But this weekend? You're on."

Paige laughed and leaned back onto his shoulder. She didn't care what they did, as long as they got to spend the day together. "I think I have an idea," she finally said, grabbing his arm and dragging him back into the house. She could tell that he wanted to dig in his heels, but he was a good sport and followed her up the stairs and into her studio.

"Please, no," Bryce said. Sometimes, when she worked late into the night, he'd sit in the armchair behind her and watch her paint. Today, that was going to change.

"You've seen the business side of things," Paige said. "Now it's time to see my side."

"Paige, I don't have a creative bone in my body. Maybe when it comes to mixing drinks, but not this." He stood there and allowed Paige to wrap an apron around him, but kept making uncomfortable noises.

"You'll be fine," she assured him. "We're just playing around, okay? Don't take it so seriously." She picked up one of the half-finished canvases and placed it on the easel before them. There were faded squares of pastel colors blended together along the top, but the bottom half was completely empty.

"Oh, no," Bryce said, holding his hands in front of him. "I am *not* messing up one of your paintings."

"It's fine." Paige rolled her eyes. "I did this last night in no time. Grab a brush and we'll get started."

Bryce looked around at the cups of brushes scattered around the room. "Can we start with something easier?"

"Okay, choose a color." Paige kicked a tub of acrylic paints over to him.

"That's not any easier." He picked up a tube covered with dark green and blue paint. "How do I know which color is which?"

She took it from him and flipped the cap open. "It's red," she deadpanned.

"Ah. And so clearly labeled for my convenience."

"You can't label art," she said dramatically. She dug through another box of palettes before choosing one with a dozen paint wells. "Pick a few more. We're gonna need a lot of colors for this."

Paige continued gathering brushes and cloths, opening the window to let the cool breeze in. Bryce squeezed — in Paige's humble opinion — conservative amounts of paint onto the palette at random.

"Where do we start?" he asked. Bryce stood with his palette in hand, wearing only the stained apron and a pair of joggers. His bed head hadn't been brushed and, funniest of all, he looked like a deer caught in headlights.

"Don't be scared," Paige said. She took his hand and pressed a large sponge roller into his palm. "You can start wherever you want."

"With this?" Now, he was even more worried.

Paige situated herself behind Bryce, turning him so that he faced the canvas, and guided his arm. They pressed the sponge against the stark canvas, and she allowed him to move freely. "Don't worry about making it perfect," she instructed. "And don't worry about messing up."

Bryce began to apply paint with more confidence, while Paige grabbed her favorite flat brush and joined him. She allowed him to work at his own pace, enjoying the look of concentration he wore. She studied him, soon noticing a playful smile on his lips and the way his blue eyes scanned the canvas. It was all so captivating that she couldn't stop staring.

"What?" he asked, his smile widening.

"Nothing," she said with a shake of her head. "I'm happy to be here…with you." They worked in silence for a few more minutes before Paige remembered her news.

"Clint and Kindall have set a date," Paige said. "We'll be going to Texas in May, if you want to come as my plus-one."

"Of course. Are you excited to be going home so soon?"

"I am," Paige said. "It'll be good to see everyone again. And it'll be the first time that Jade, Clint and I will have been together in person since Jade's wedding." She let her arm fall to her side, not caring about the paint smudge that was no doubt on her leg. "It really is ending, isn't it? We're all growing up."

"Beginning," Bryce corrected. "You can grow apart from your friends, but that doesn't mean it's over. And who decided what growing up is supposed to be to begin with? Who decided what getting your life together entails? I'm perfectly happy doing what I love with the person I love, and that's all that should matter."

"You're right." She began painting again. "And Jade will have had her baby by then. We can look after him and, oh, you can meet my parents, too."

"Slow down," he said sternly. "Let's get through the year without killing each other first." Bryce's side of the canvas was overtaken with orange shapes over a background of seafoam green. There were patches of blue and white as well, but at least he was following her advice and playing around.

"Are you sure about all of this?" Paige asked, a bit of her old insecurities creeping in. "About the community center and this place and…me?"

"I love you, Paige," he said, putting down his brush and facing her. "I would have thought I'd told you enough times that you wouldn't have to ask."

"I do believe you," she assured him. "It's just—"

Bryce dropped the palette, sending paint in every direction. Luckily, the damage was mostly to the sheets and below the knee. Bryce stared down at the mess like he wasn't sure what to do about it.

"I am so sorry," he said, pausing between each word to emphasize his point.

"It happens," Paige said with a laugh. "Why do you think I put these sheets down to begin with? I guess it's a good thing I wore shorts."

"I'll clean this up, I swear."

"I told you not to worry about it." Paige lifted his head to look at her. She still wasn't the best at flirting but, after being around Bryce for so long, she liked to think she was getting better. "How about we switch focus?"

"What did you have in mind this time?" he asked, sounding much more interested than he had when she'd suggested painting.

"How about we go by Slice of Lime for lunch," she said, trailing her hands up his sides languidly.

"That's...not what I was expecting you to say."

"Well, we'll obviously have to get cleaned up first." She slipped her fingers into the waistband of his sweats. "Race you to the showers?"

A light sparked behind Bryce's eyes, and he blessed her with a crooked smile. "You know how much I love a challenge."

Chapter Twenty

January 2

Bryce paced the white tiled floors, his hands twisting in front of him as he stared blankly ahead.

"Please, sit down," Paige said, gesturing to the empty spot on the couch next to her.

"We should probably leave," he said with his eyes on the wall above her. "We've been here since yesterday. We don't know when they'll be out or anything." His voice was shaky. "I'm sure everything's okay. These things take time. We're in the way out here."

"We're not in the way." She leaned back, her own foot tapping the floor. "Come on, you're acting worse than Spencer, and it's not your baby."

"Hey, I take my role as godfather very seriously." He stopped suddenly, looking over at Paige with a seriousness expression. "Maybe I should force my way in there and get some answers."

"Clearly, you've lost your mind." She patted the seat next to her and Bryce finally dropped into it. "We're going to stay right here until someone comes out."

In truth, Paige was just as nervous, but one of them had to hold it together. Paige and Bryce were in town for the holidays and had dropped by the penthouse when Jade's water had broken. Spencer had been in a meeting, one that he'd quickly abandoned as soon as he saw the group through the conference room window. With him leading the way, they'd made it to the private hospital where Jade would finally have little Timothy Alexander.

But that was yesterday. Paige and Bryce had slept in their waiting room and the last thing they'd heard was when Spencer had popped his head in around midnight to let them know they were going to have to induce labor. As each hour ticked by, Paige grew more and more concerned. There had been complications early in Jade's pregnancy, and that wasn't something she'd forgotten.

Bryce's leg began to bounce, shaking the couch to the point that she wished he'd start pacing again. They both jumped up at the sound of the doorknob turning. A doctor with vibrant red hair came inside and immediately turned around.

"I'm sorry, wrong room," she said, quickly shutting the door behind her.

"This is cruel," Bryce groaned, falling back onto the couch.

Paige huffed, ready to join him, when the door opened again. This time, it was Spencer, his smile radiant enough to light the room without help from the window. His suit had been dismantled in the night, and he looked like he could use a nap.

"Spence," Bryce said, rushing over to hug his brother. "I take it we have good news?"

Spencer could only nod as breathy laughs escaped his lips. "The best news," he finally said. "It wasn't easy, but Jade is perfect, and Timmy..." Tears sprang into his eyes and his voice cracked with a sob. "He's the most beautiful thing I've ever seen."

Bryce held Spencer as he cried. Paige stayed back, finally able to breathe. She was loath to admit it, but she had been scared. Her hands began to shake, and she hid them behind her so that no one would see.

"Do you want to see him?" Spencer asked.

"What kind of question is that?" Paige said in mock annoyance. "I wanted to see him months ago."

She and Bryce linked their fingers together and followed Spencer from the room.

"When will Mom and Dad get here?" Bryce asked. "And Jade's parents?"

"They'll be coming in together," Spencer explained. "They're on their way now, but the traffic from the hangar is murder today."

There was another set of doors and a hallway to go down before they came to Jade's room. It was cool inside, with a sitting area and flowers on every surface. The private birthing room was nothing like the sterile white hospital rooms Paige was accustomed to. Jade was lying on a hospital bed across the room, an IV to one side and a heart monitor on the other. To have been through what she had, she looked amazing.

"At least we know I'll be able to fit in my dress by May," Jade said with a weary smile.

"Nobody was worried about that," Paige said, squatting next to the bed. "How are you feeling?"

"The doctor says I'll be weak for a while, but I'll be all right otherwise." Her eyes trailed over to the clear crib in the corner of the room and Paige's gaze followed. Spencer was the first to cross over to the crib and pick up a small blue bundle.

"Impossibly small," Paige muttered out loud. Bryce was by her side, an arm over her shoulders. Spencer placed the swaddling into Jade's waiting arms, so gently, like he might break it. She arranged the blankets, tucking here and folding there, until Paige could see bright blue-green eyes staring up in amazement.

Timothy was all pink wrinkles and dark wisps of hair. His mouth opened wide and he began to cry, his eyes disappearing into the creases. Paige laughed, warm tears spilling onto her cheeks. She felt Bryce's grip tighten, and Paige saw that he was crying, too.

"You were right, Spence," he said. "He's the most beautiful thing in this world." He leaned in closer. "I'm your Uncle Bryce. And I'll make sure you get plenty of girlfriends."

Spencer reached over to swat his arm but, interestingly enough, Timothy had stopped crying.

"Go on," Jade said to Paige. "Introduce yourself."

Paige looked down at the squirming boy, his eyes darting everywhere until he seemed to focus on her. "I'm your Auntie Paige," she said quietly. "And I already love you so much." She had so much she wanted to tell him, that she wanted to tell everyone, but there would be time for that later. For now, she was content just to watch the little miracle in Jade's arms and let him know that he was loved.

A knock on the door drew their attention away from the baby. Paige expected the Alexanders to be there but was shocked when Clint and Kindall came into the room.

"You didn't think we'd miss this, did you?" Clint asked, slightly offended. He and Kindall had their hands clasped together, her emerald engagement ring catching the light.

"I can't believe y'all made it," Jade said. "And you beat my parents."

"Not by much," Victoria said. Both sets of parents — now grandparents — stepped inside.

Their eyes shone with unshed tears, and they beamed in a way that one only saw when a new life entered the world. After hugs and congratulations were exchanged, they huddled around the bed, forming a cocoon around the new mother. She was sure they were breaking some sort of rule with as many people as there were in the room, but Paige couldn't be bothered to worry about it.

"Everyone's here," Jade said with disbelief.

"We need a photo," Bryce said, taking out his phone and positioning the camera above them. Jade tried to flatten her hair with her free hand, but Spencer had already grabbed it. They all smiled up at the camera while Bryce counted down.

Paige could see them all on the screen as Bryce tapped the shutter button — every person who she cared about more than anything else. This was her life, her family — and it wasn't perfect by any means. But wasn't that the point?

Want to see more like this?
Here's a taster for you to enjoy!

Single in Seattle: A Latte of Love
Gloria Herrmann

Excerpt

"I think we got it," Molly said confidently to the almost naked man standing in the corner, wearing nothing but a stark white towel draped across his tan waist.

"You sure?"

Molly nodded as she scrutinized her work. "Yeah, the lighting was brilliant. I don't think we could have done any better."

"If you say so. You're the expert with that thing." The model pointed at the large camera Molly cradled in her hands, the screen displaying the digital shots from the day of working with him.

Molly loved her job as a professional photographer. Her friends were insanely jealous. What woman wouldn't be? She spent her days in her studio behind the lens of her trusty camera, capturing sexy images of some of the most gorgeous men from all over the world. Either she was paid to travel to them or they flew to Seattle to have her work her magic. Authors in the romance industry adored her photos. Her attention to detail had won her awards over the years, but what she loved the most was bringing the characters from books alive. Sure, it didn't hurt to look at well-defined muscles and sculpted abs that begged to be touched and to know what was hidden beneath the scrap of cloth that usually covered these men, but that wasn't how the business worked. Her friends would argue it was just because Molly didn't throw herself at these scantily clad men that she was missing out on these valuable opportunities.

If they only knew how nervous most of these men were, their fragile egos stripped down for her. It took Molly the first half of the shoot to calm them, easing them out of their shells, getting them just to loosen up enough for the right shot. It was more like babysitting rather than staring at a buffet, despite what her best friends thought. Not all the models lacked self-confidence, however. There were some who would stroll in, look directly into the camera and own it. But, for the most part, a lot of the guys were unsure and needed coaxing. Molly often felt more like a counselor than the world-famous photographer that she was.

Today, the Seattle sun was shielded behind soft, white clouds, filtering its rays into her studio that overlooked the Puget Sound. Her tall, glass windows provided the most stunning views of the shimmering water and the bustling city. Molly had worked hard for this view. It hadn't come easy or cheap — or without her busting her ass to make her name known in the photography industry. She had the scars — mostly emotional, but scars, nonetheless — to prove the struggles she'd endured, climbing to the top. Now she was one of the most sought-after photographers. Models from all over the globe wanted her to shoot them. *New York Times* and *USA Today* bestselling authors and publishers almost begged for her to shoot their covers. They wanted the best and...well, Molly was. Her skills proved that she had something special and everyone knew it.

Not bothering to sit down at her desk—bending over, instead—to focus on the images she was uploading to her laptop to edit, she almost forgot to say goodbye to the model she had just worked with. It wasn't until he was standing close to her, now fully dressed, that she realized he was still in her studio. Having him near her like that shifted the atmosphere in the room. His dominating presence was invading her space, creating nervous waves in her stomach. She inhaled his expensive aftershave, looked up from her screen and smiled.

Molly managed to say, "Great shoot today. Thanks again."

Remember to breathe, Molly.

"Yeah, it was amazing. You're amazing." The man paused, running his fingers along his day-old beard, the perfect blend of refined and unkempt sexy. His voice was silky and oozed well-practiced enticement. Molly watched him stand still, contemplating his next move. She was tempted to grab her camera and snap another shot. The light was hitting him just right and his pose was thoughtful and natural. This man was gorgeous.

He turned his mesmerizing gaze toward her and asked, "Do you want to grab a drink?"

Molly swallowed. It wasn't the first time she had been asked out by a model after a shoot. Sometimes it was the result of having bonded over their frail vulnerabilities. Sometimes they figured she was as good a lay as any while they were in town—another stamp in their romantic passport, so to speak. Molly wasn't so sure about this one. He wasn't overly emotional or guarded about his body, nor did he seem to really desire her. *So, what is he after?* She watched him scan the large studio. There was her answer. This type of square footage didn't come cheap and he knew that.

"You know, maybe another time. I'm really excited to get this edited." Molly pointed at her sleek silver laptop, delivering a fake smile in hopes it would put him off.

He nodded and thanked her again as he saw himself out. *The nerve.* Molly rolled her eyes and released the air she had been holding in her lungs. While she was in mid sigh, her cell phone chirped.

"Hello," she answered, a little more gruffly than she'd intended.

"Wow, so what's with the 'tude, lady? Bad day?"

It was one of her best friends, Tiffany.

"Just got done working with a model."

"Well, then why do you sound all cranky? Was he awful? So good-looking that you couldn't handle it?" Tiffany teased, causing Molly to laugh and her mood to lighten.

"You know the type. He wanted to go out for drinks—"

Tiffany cut her off quickly. "And you said, yes, right? Because if you didn't, you honestly need to have your head examined."

"I'd have to say he was more interested in my real estate than me." Molly frowned.

"Like real estate, as in the prime location between your legs? You know, it's all about location, location, location, baby."

"I wish." Molly huffed in frustration. "No, more like the prime location of my studio."

"That sucks."

"Tell me about it. He was gorgeous and he smelled divine. He was totally your type—tall, dark and devilishly handsome."

She heard Tiffany's disappointment through the phone. "Really? Oh, I just don't know how you do it, Molly. I have to give it to you. I would simply come undone working with those gorgeous men and not taking advantage of them every chance I got."

Tiffany always acted like she was some aggressive sex kitten, but they knew the truth. She was actually quite timid, which was a huge reason why she was single. All three of them were single and not dating anyone special. It didn't usually work that they were unattached all at the same time, but they were now. Their other best friend, Mackenzie, was the mother hen of the group. Well, more like the bossy one—completely overbearing, but with an absolute heart of gold. She, too, teased Molly about her line of work, but Mackenzie loved being a teacher, as it helped fill her maternal void. They had biological clocks that had gone haywire over the last couple of years, but everyone had warned them as they entered the dirty thirties that baby fever would hit soon after, and it had for Tiffany and Mackenzie. Every time they passed a stroller, neither could resist the temptation of peering in to catch a glimpse of some infant swaddled in fuzzy pink or blue blankets. Molly? She had her moments. They were brief and passed quickly when she heard the wail of a newborn or the shrill sound of a tantrum from a toddler. That didn't tempt her to want to rent out her womb for nine months.

She looked at her spotless, chic studio. Her smile went deep into her soul, masking the want for a baby. Her space sparkled and gleamed with the afternoon

Seattle sunlight, illuminating sleek lines and utterly contemporary taste.

If she were being completely honest with herself, yes, she did indeed want a child, eventually. But Molly also realized she was missing a very important part of the equation—a man. She didn't want just a sperm donor, though she and her friends had discussed that over far too much wine and Chinese food one night, considering it as a last resort. That had left them laughing for hours. No, Molly wanted the real deal. They all did. They wanted a man—a sexy, successful and simply wonderful man. *Is that really asking for too much?*

Being single, especially in Seattle, came with its challenges. Molly thought the enormous Emerald City should be plentiful with eligible bachelors, but Molly assumed that, as with any place, being single was a mixture of bad luck and an overly detailed list of the personality traits she wanted in a boyfriend. As time passed, her list had grown a lot shorter. She'd crossed off quite a few of her must-haves and was looking to review her available options. Now she figured it was mainly the bad luck that was keeping her single. Molly had been unattached the longest out of her friends, who were more like her sisters. Tiffany had been on a dating spree recently, but Mackenzie and Molly had known that none of the guys were Mr. Right for their friend. Mackenzie also had a pretty extensive list of requirements for her ideal mate, and she was even more stubborn than Molly when it came to sacrificing the qualities she was willing to live with, so she dated very little.

"Well, since you didn't want drinks with that sexy model, how about meeting up with us?" Tiffany asked.

Molly smiled. Yes, a drink with her best pals she could do. "That sounds lovely, actually." She could use some cheering up. The best cure for her bruised ego was some quality time with her besties.

"Great. I'll pick up Mac and we'll swing by the studio and grab ya. Sound good?"

"Perfect. I have some edits I want to go through, so just buzz when you guys get here."

Molly said goodbye and hung up. She stared at the monitor in front of her, the images of the model in various poses looking back her.

* * * *

Lost in her work tweaking the images with an array of filters, Molly was so engrossed that she almost didn't hear the loud buzzing that echoed off the large studio walls. She got up quickly from her desk and jogged to the massive double doors to let her friends in.

"Jeesh, what were you doing? I have been ringing that dang buzzer for, like, *forever*," Tiffany complained as she slipped past Molly into the studio. Mackenzie frowned and hugged Molly.

"We've only been standing outside the door for a minute," Mackenzie assured her.

Tiffany walked over to one of the large windows facing the Puget Sound. The sun was setting, casting a tangerine hue over the haze of the city. "God, do you ever get tired of this magnificent view?"

Molly shook her head as she joined her, staring out at the glittery lights in the surrounding buildings that seemed to stretch up toward the sky. "Nope."

"Yeah, I didn't think so." Tiffany laughed as she faced Molly. Her dark hair was loose on her thin shoulders. Tiffany's large eyes were a soulful brown and she had the best cheekbones. Tiffany was gorgeous in a unique and completely unexpected way. Molly's brain acted as a camera, capturing shots of her friend's delicate features as the sunset cast a shadowy light on her face. Tiffany sensed what Molly was doing and threw her a pouty look.

Mackenzie stood next them. The willowy blonde towered over Molly, making her feel short and stubby. Mackenzie had the figure of a teenager, slim and athletic. Her sun-kissed hair was cut in a sleek bob, framing the sharp angles of her face. She was another beautiful woman. Molly couldn't help but snap mental pictures of Mackenzie, too. She searched Molly curiously with soft mocha eyes. They all had brown eyes in varied shades of the common color, but resembling their different tastes in coffee. Tiffany had the espresso, dark and bold. Mackenzie was more of an iced mocha with an extra shot. Molly's resembled the instant crap coffee variety that no one really liked. Molly hated her eyes. They were plain. Her friends had tried to convince her otherwise, but they both had spectacular depth and richness in theirs. Molly thought hers looked like a muddy puddle after a typical downpour in Seattle — watery, with a sad, muted tone. Nothing special.

"What's going on with you?" Mackenzie reached for Molly, concern swimming in her eyes and worry creasing her otherwise wrinkle-free face, the result of fabulous genetics.

Molly sighed. *Is there anything going on with me?* They usually accused her of being moody, but she was an artist. *Isn't that sort of the job description? Acting the part of the tortured soul?* They sure never let her play that role for very long.

Tiffany stared at her hard and added, "Yeah, you seemed cranky on the phone. So what's up?"

"I don't know. I mean..." Molly really couldn't explain how she felt. She had a blessed life. Granted, she had worked for it, but, regardless, she knew she was lucky. Happy? Well, that was a different ball of wax.

"Drinks. That's what we need." Tiffany perked up, her hand on her hip, taking a sassy stance. She reached for the oversized purse that was slung over her shoulder. A Louis Vuitton knock-off, but it looked as real as they came. It was their little secret. Tiffany dug around and retrieved a bottle of Prosecco, holding it up for them to all gaze at her prize.

"You were carrying that in there? Oh dear. Seriously, Tiffany," Mackenzie scolded.

Tiffany winked and answered with a wicked grin.

"I, for one, am thrilled our friend is lugging around a bottle. You never know when you may need it." Molly grinned happily at Tiffany. "It does make you look a little like a wino, but you're my favorite drunk."

"No, you have me mistaken. I'm fun, not a drunk." Tiffany defended as she moved toward a long table that was against the wall opposite the windows. "Besides, at least I bring the good stuff."

"I have an idea. Let's stay in. Want to order some food?" Mackenzie suggested.

"Yes, let's do that. Molly's got one of the best views in all of Seattle. Let's just hang out here," Tiffany replied while she peeled the label away to get to the cork.

"Chinese?" Mackenzie whipped out her cell phone and started to dial their favorite takeout.

"Hell, yes," Molly and Tiffany answered in unison.

These were her girls. It didn't matter if they stayed in or went out on the town. As long as they were together, they were guaranteed to have fun.

Shortly, they were seated around a large glass table that Molly normally used to lay out prints from shoots. They dined on their fill of chow mein, pork fried rice and more Kung Pao shrimp than any woman should ever eat. White cartons, soy sauce packets and chopsticks were littered around them as they chatted about everything—mostly about the lack of sex or romance in their lives. Biting into a crispy fortune cookie—her favorite—Molly surveyed her beautiful friends. She couldn't understand why any of them were single. Tiffany was gorgeous, sweet and sassy... What was there not to love about her? Mackenzie was stunning, witty and full of love... She had so much to offer. Then there was her. She knew she might not be the sexiest thing on the planet, but she was successful, caring and everyone constantly complimented her on how pleasant she was, even telling her she was sort of hot, especially when she wore her glasses. *So how is it that I haven't landed the perfect guy yet?* Cracking open another cookie, she read the thin slip of white paper. Bold red font stared back at her, reading, *'There is nothing truer than the company of friends.'* How right is that fortune?

More wine flowed and, to keep the mood light, Molly blasted the radio. She and her two best friends danced barefoot in the empty studio, singing their hearts out and putting on a drunken performance that could rival the best pop star's. Tiffany swayed her hips to the song. Mackenzie took a while to loosen up, but then started to bop to the beat. Molly busted out some goofy moves that reminded her of middle school dances, her favorite being the 'running man'. They laughed hard, clutching their sides when Tiffany took a spill on the slippery wood floor. In their feeble attempt at helping her up, they all ended up on the floor somehow, spread-eagled, staring up at the vaulted ceilings. Music continued to play, filling the wide and open space, but the mood had shifted. That was when the laughter died and the deep realness of their friendship was exposed.

"I love you, guys," Tiffany whispered, her dark tresses fanned out against the honey-colored bamboo floor.

"Me too," Mackenzie added softly.

Molly tried to swallow the lump that was forming in her throat, feeling tears starting to surface. "I love you both. Thank you for tonight."

They all stayed on the floor, listening to several more songs before Tiffany said, "God, this floor is killing my back. I feel old."

Mackenzie and Molly both laughed.

"And for the record, we *are* old," Mackenzie replied.

"I wanted to say the same thing, but figured I would tough it out until one of you cracked." Molly started to get up.

Mackenzie and Tiffany groaned as they eased themselves off the floor. Working quietly as a team, they cleaned up the remnants of their dinner.

"I would totally live here, Molly," Mackenzie commented as she tossed several cartons into a waste basket.

Tiffany was wiping up some sticky Kung Pao sauce. "Seriously. This studio is so fabulous. You need to let me move in here."

"I do love this place." Molly looked around at her kingdom. An enormous clear-glass shelf that held her many awards was against one of the walls. Expensive frames that contained some of her best work were hung precisely in the perfect locations. Various shades, light fixtures and tons of other photography gear were set up in one corner. The room celebrated her. It showcased all of her efforts but, more importantly, it proudly displayed her passion for this form of art.

After every last morsel was cleaned and the work space was back to being immaculate, they made their way back to the window. The sun had long since disappeared, leaving the city lights to twinkle silently as the three of them stared out at the busy traffic below.

"Thank you again, guys. I really needed this tonight."

Mackenzie and Tiffany linked their arms through hers as she stood in the middle.

She would be lost without them. They knew all her secrets and her fears. They had supported her during her moments of crippling self-doubt. They'd loved her when she was at her worst. They'd dried her tears when critics had given her harsh reviews. They were her cheerleaders. They'd pushed her to continue to pursue her dream so many times when she'd just wanted to give up. They had been the first to celebrate when she finally did become successful and had told her countless times how much she deserved it.

These women were more than just friends. They were her tribe, her sisters. They were Molly's everything.

About the Author

Lori Fayre was born and raised in a small South Georgia town. An obsessive consumer of romance throughout all media, she knew that it was the only genre she could ever write. Love should always be full of passion and adventure, and Lori proves as much in her novels that span multiple genres and pairings. When she's not writing love stories, she enjoys reading, sketching, and spending time with her husband and Yorkie.

Lori loves to hear from readers. You can find her contact information, website details and author profile page at https://www.totallybound.com

Home of Erotic Romance

Sign up for our newsletter and find out about all our romance book releases, eBook sales and promotions, sneak peeks and FREE romance books!